MISSING, BELIEVED CRAZY

Terence Blacker is the author of many novels for young readers, including *The Transfer*, *Paro̶̶̶̶*, award-winning *Boy2Girl*. He songs, and lives in a house which he converted from a go

Praise for Teren̶ ̶̶̶̶̶er

Missing, Believed Crazy:

'Entertaining and cleverly constructed, it's enjoyable for the way the narratives of the five distinct and characterful protagonists are interwoven, and for its subtly mounting tension' *Sunday Times*

'Blacker cleverly caters to children's appetites for celebrity culture while allowing them to discover the sour taste for themselves' *Sunday Telegraph*

Boy2Girl:

'This fast-paced story is a roller coaster of hilarious incidents' *Mail on Sunday*

'Hugely funny, then painfully affecting . . . offers genuine insights amongst the laughter' *Guardian*

The Angel Factory:

'A gripping and dramatic adventure involving high technology, deception, intrigue and even murder. Terence Blacker's direct style makes the sinister proje̶ of *The Angel Factory* seem disturbingly poss̶̶

'Well written and pacy, this is a story that ju̶ finished' *Independent*

Terence  Blacker

MISSING, BELIEVED CRAZY

MACMILLAN CHILDREN'S BOOKS

First published 2009 by Macmillan Children's Books

This edition published 2010 by Macmillan Children's Books,
a division of Macmillan Publishers Limited
20 New Wharf Road, London N1 9RR
Basingstoke and Oxford
Associated companies throughout the world
www.panmacmillan.com

ISBN 978-0-330-45849-8

1 3 5 7 9 8 6 4 2

A CIP catalogue record for this book is available from
the British Library.

Typeset by Intype Libra Limited
Printed and bound in the UK by CPI Mackays, Chatham ME5 8TD

To Valerie Christie, a superb librarian

TJB.

Trix.

Trixie.

Beatrix.

Little Trixie.

Tragic Trixie.

The Trixter.

Erica Jane.

Sometimes it is difficult to remember who she was, the real Trix Johansson-Bell.

Late at night, when I can't get to sleep, I look through the mementoes of Trix that I keep in a suitcase beneath my bed. There is a catapult, some photographs, a torn T-shirt with 'Feed the World' on the front. There are newspaper cuttings with headlines like 'WHERE IS LITTLE TRIXIE?', 'TRIXIE'S CHATROOM SECRET', 'TRAGIC TRIXIE: SHE CARED THAT WE DIDN'T CARE' and 'WHO HAS GOT MY LITTLE ANGEL? PLEADS ACTRESS'.

They make me miss her, but the Trix I knew is nowhere there.

There are only four other people who know the truth about that summer. The gang. The group. The oddest bunch of teenagers who have ever come together to commit a crime. Take a look and see what you think.

JADE HART. American, tall, good-looking, a supermodel of the future (according to Jade Hart). Very popular with the boys and best friend of –

HOLLY DE VRIESS. Strong, badly dressed and always in a hurry. Ever since she took on one of the boys at arm-wrestling and won, they call her 'the Hulk' – but not to her face. Very popular with the teachers and one-time enemy of –

MARK BLISS. Floppy-haired, sporty and with the kind of posh accent that makes you want to throw something. Mark fancied himself as one of the cool guys. Very popular with virtually everyone in our year except –

Me. WILLIAM CHURCH, better known as 'Wiki', ever since someone decided that I knew so much about stuff that I was like a walking Wikipedia. Mark would call me 'brother' in a way that was not racist but wasn't exactly friendly either. In spite of the colour of my skin – I'm one of the few black kids at our private school, Cathcart College – I am Mr Unnoticed. If I have a talent, it is for being anonymous. In any group photograph, I am the one standing half-hidden at the back. I can walk into a room and no one will know I am there.

Yet there we were, the Trixter's gang: Trix, Jade, Holly, Mark and Wiki. For one summer, it was us against the world. Our lives revolved around an event – a crime, you could say – that we codenamed 'The Vanish'.

The date of The Vanish we called 'V Day'.

WIKI

Take a deep breath. It is the first day of the Summer Term at Cathcart College. This is the place where parents who can afford it send their boys and girls to board between the ages of thirteen and seventeen. It is in sweeping grounds (a wood, a science block, a cricket pitch with a pavilion – the works) at the end of a long drive. As school returns, a great army of 4x4s trundle down the drive, kicking up dust. It is like a war, an invasion – The Invasion of the Rich and Anxious Parents.

Cathcart likes to pretend it has a history. It has a Latin motto, 'Vade in Victoria', which means something like 'Win Everything You Can', a lame school song, its own old-fashioned language (our class is called 'the Remove' for reasons no one has ever understood) and a headmaster, Mr Griffiths – also know as 'Griffo', 'the Griffon' and a few other names you don't want to know about. When you first arrive at Cathcart, the Griffon gives you a little talk about how Cathcartians (sorry, that's what they call us) are special. 'Cathcart College will give you the engine to take you through life,' he says. 'If you were a car, a Cathcartian might be a Ferrari or a nippy little luxury BMW. Some of you might be a top-of-the-range Aston Martin. What you will not be – and I can promise you this, Cathcartians – is a Ford Mondeo.'

I had heard these words during my first week at

4

Cathcart and at that moment I wanted the earth to open and swallow me up. I was convinced that somehow the Head had seen me arriving at college for the first time and had discovered my terrible secret: my parents drive a Mondeo.

MR NIGEL 'GRIFFO' GRIFFITHS

I regret that I am unable to comment on the events leading up to the disappearance of our former pupil Beatrix Johansson-Bell. I should point out however that the event occurred during the summer holidays and the college had no control over the behaviour of her and other Cathcart pupils at that time.

Cathcart has an excellent record of academic and sporting achievement and has risen steadily in the league of top independent schools. We pride ourselves on being a caring school. I will be making no further statements.

WIKI

At Cathcart, what your parents do – how famous they are, how much money they have, whether they're generally cool or not – is a sort of currency. My mother's a librarian, my father an accountant. No one has ever heard of them. At Cathcart, that makes me a pauper, invisible. Trix Johansson-Bell was in the millionaire class. Her mum was an actress and looked like she could be Trix's better-looking older sister. Her stepdad was a sports agent who hung out with footballers, tennis-players, motor-racing drivers and so on.

Trix was one of the cool crowd – she went around with bouncy, super-confident Holly de Vriess and pretty, look-at-me-everyone Jade Hart. Later, when I saw more of her, I realized that Trix was always slightly out of place at Cathcart. She had short dark hair and the face of someone you just knew was stronger than her skinny frame suggested.

She was like an angry pixie. A very angry pixie.

JADE

What made Trix angry? Most everything. When the sun was shining, and some great music was playing on the radio and the world seemed kind of all right for a few seconds, she would be the one to point out that the food we had just bought from the school shop could keep an African village going for a week, or ask whether we realized that 5.67 million children (or was 7.56?) went to bed hungry every night.

I mean, bring us down, why don't you?

I'm not saying these things aren't important but there's a time and a place, right? Trix was just *so* inappropriate sometimes.

HOLLY

I had no closer friend but, between you and me, the way Trix decorated her room that first day of term was borderline creepy. During the holidays, she had collected all these photographs and posters of starving children in

Africa, with swollen stomachs and flies around their big hungry eyes. Most of us put cheerful things on our walls – pictures of whales and film stars and (if you're Jade) boy bands – but not good old Trix. She had to transform her room into a mini-museum of world misery.

WIKI

During the Easter holidays, there had been one of those big TV charity appeals where newsreaders show off in tights and rich pop stars tell everyone that we should be giving our money away to charity. Trix's mum, the famous actress, had taken part in some fashion event, which had raised a whole load of cash.

It did something – sent Trix slightly mad. When she came back to Cathcart, she could talk of nothing else but how privileged we all were, how we were just a bunch of rich kids (speak for yourself, Trix), how we had to do something.

Make a difference, she said. It was up to us to make a difference.

JADE

I blame Miss Fothergill. It was in her first citizenship class of that term that the summer's big bad idea first came up. A charity fashion show at school.

Charity? Fashion? Cathcart? Only Trix could believe that was going to work.

MISS FOTHERGILL

In the past, Cathcartians have not had the best reputation when it comes to responsible behaviour. Some of the older children were a little bit rough (bullying would be too strong a word) towards the new arrivals. A rather disastrous story about sixth-formers visiting pubs had appeared in the Sunday papers.

Morality is important – particularly for children who are lucky enough to be at a private school. I suggested to the headmaster that once a week I would take the Remove for citizenship classes.

Trix Johansson-Bell loved those classes. She led the discussions, full of ideas and information. When it came to the ethical life, she was a model pupil.

I wanted a value-led project for that term. It was a time of exams and pressure. The children, I thought, would benefit from giving something back to those less fortunate than themselves. The idea that Trix came up with during citizenship class – a fashion show to raise money for Africa – seemed to me an excellent one.

Sadly I overestimated the Cathcartian spirit of generosity.

MARK

Miss Fothergill and Trix – what a couple they made. A former nun and the class keenie. Together, they were an accident waiting to happen.

WIKI

Miss Fothergill was an oddity at Cathcart. She was beautiful enough, in a pale, shy way, for about sixty per cent of the boys at the school to be deeply in love with her, but she dressed as if her clothes came from charity shops and car boot sales. She never mentioned her family, and when someone asked her anything about her own life in class, she quickly changed the subject. Some of the most important words in the Cathcart dictionary – Nike, Lexus, iPhone, Rolex, Dior – meant nothing to her. She drove a small, tinny car and, on the rare occasions that she became slightly angry, she would say, 'Jiminy Crickets!' or 'Glory be, child!' or sometimes 'Phooey!'

She had once been a nun, or so the rumour went. There were a number of theories about why she had left a place where all was peaceful, holy and innocent (a convent) to teach at a place where all was noisy, grabby and selfish (Cathcart College):

1. She had fallen madly in love with 'Bony' Spratt, the sports master, or possibly 'Dodgy' Davis, a geography master, or even Griffo himself. There was no evidence for any of these ideas, although someone once thought they saw the Griffon touching her back as she walked through a door.

2. She had a sacred mission to bring the word of God to a group of privileged kids at a lame boarding school.

3. While she was in the convent, she had become pregnant by a monk and had to leave in order to have their secret love child. One day that child would be educated at Cathcart. Miss Fothergill is in her thirties and so the word is that quite soon a boy or girl will arrive looking spookily like her. Every year, there are rumours that Miss Fothergill's secret love child has arrived at last but the general feeling is that he/she is not yet among us.

None of these theories quite explained why Miss Fothergill was at Cathcart College or why she was mad enough to try to teach the Remove how to be good citizens. We were at that dangerous stage, having been at Cathcart long enough to have lost the fear that we had in our first year, but not long enough to start worrying about exams or the future. We were ready to test our power over adults.

HOLLY

Trix must have talked to Miss Fothergill about the TV charity event because, in her first lesson, Miss Fothergill brought up the subject of raising money for good causes.

'Now,' she said in that breezy Mary Poppins way of hers, 'what could we, in our own little way, do to help the poor and underprivileged – do our bit to save the world from starvation?'

There was the usual silence. Then up went a hand. It was Trix.

'We could put on our own event – a sponsored charity fashion show.'

'Very good, Trix,' said Miss Fothergill.

It was a set-up, if ever I saw one.

At first no one was keen. But Trix was on a roll. She went to the front of the class and talked about this village, Mwanduna, in Mali. If the Remove at Cathcart adopted it, they could have a well, books, food. 'I've worked out that, if we could just raise, say, three hundred pounds, we could feed twenty children for a year. We might even be able to buy a cow for a dairy farmer out there.'

There was nervous laughter in the class.

'No, but seriously, listen . . .'

And Trix started explaining how it could work, how we could have a good time and help feed starving African children. Gradually people began to pay attention.

We talked about the fashion show and suddenly it began to seem like fun. The girls could parade up and down in their best clothes. Jade and a few others began to look interested. A gang of boys at the back of the class suddenly seemed to think it was a good idea too.

MARK

My mate Tom Parkinson put up his hand.

'Would you be one of the models, Miss Fothergill?' he asked in his best husky, tough-boy way. 'I'd really like to sponsor you.'

Miss Fothergill actually blushed.

'Don't be silly, Tom,' she said.

'But I thought you wanted to save the world,' said Tom. 'Make a difference, like. You could be a supermodel.'

And suddenly we're all joining in from the back. 'Go on, miss. Make a difference.'

Miss Fothergill was losing it. She didn't want to squash the idea and she sure as hell didn't want to be a model.

'The details of this event will be decided by its organizers. Trix, clearly you must be involved. Who will be helping you?'

Trix looked around. 'Holly,' she said. 'And Jade would be good.'

JADE

Oh, terrific. Thanks a bunch, Trix.

HOLLY

I'm all for charity but I really, really wasn't sure about this.

WIKI

'I think,' said Miss Fothergill, 'that there should be a male presence on the organizing committee. Don't you, boys?'

'They'll only mess it up,' said Holly.

The gang at the back were slipping down in their seats, taking care not to let the teacher catch their eye. The others didn't want to look stupid in front of the cool guys.

I looked at Trix, who was staring ahead, almost as if she was regretting it already. Miss Fothergill crossed her arms in a sort of disappointed-but-not-entirely-surprised way.

'What about Wiki, miss? I mean, William.' I turned to stare at Mark Bliss, whose idea of a joke this was.

'Why William, Mark?' Miss Fothergill asked.

'Because he's –' The class seemed to hold its breath.

'Because I'm black?' I spoke quietly.

'No, no.' The grin on Bliss's face looked strained now. Not even he could get away with racism in a citizenship class. 'I just thought he was really good at fashion.'

I turned towards Trix, my mind made up. The best way to fight prejudice is to face it head-on. Without doubt, the boys would laugh at me but right then I didn't want to have anything to do with them anyway. 'I'll help you,' I said. 'It's worth doing.'

Trix smiled. 'Thanks, Wik,' she said.

Nightmare scenario. That was all we needed. It was a lame idea. It was going to be totally embarrassing. I was going to have to put up with being one of Miss Fothergill's favourites for the next few weeks.

And now the Remove's undisputed Nerd of the Year was going to be involved.

Fact: nothing cool and good will ever involve Wiki Church.

We gave him the look, Holly and I. He just blinked and smiled, his spots glowing gently.

WIKI

That was the moment when we discovered just how determined Trix could be. Within a week of that fateful citizenship lesson, she had us all running around for an event that none of us in our hearts had wanted to happen.

Holly came up with the name the Cathcart Catwalk Charity Challenge and then started to work on a poster. She decided that a picture of a sad-looking African child was not, whatever Trix might have thought, going to sell tickets for an end-of-term event at Cathcart College. Instead, she asked me to look for a photograph of a supermodel and make her look as if she went to our school.

Easy, right?

I found a hot picture of Kate Moss and, with the help of a shot of my school tie, photo-edited her into the sexiest Cathcartian there has ever been.

Jade had been the most reluctant of us to become involved – school fashion shows were like the lamest things, she said – but she cheered up when Trix told her she could be the Catwalk Challenge's creative director. It was Jade who recruited the models from the Remove and who decided that the show would be 'a total history of fashion over the last fifty years'. She was the one who convinced those taking part in the show to raid their parents' wardrobes for historical items of fashion.

And me? I was on the sidelines, as usual. I found out

the school hall was available and convinced the school administrator that we should be allowed to hold a charity show there two days after the end of exams. I worked out how we were going to sell tickets. I came up with the idea for a raffle.

At the time, it all seemed to be going well.

MISS FOTHERGILL

I was impressed. By the time exams began in late May, Holly's rather saucy poster was all over the school. Jade had managed to persuade several of the Remove to be models. Trix was involving little William Church in some of the less glamorous details. Even at a time when the thoughts of (most!) Cathcartians were on exams, there was quite a little buzz about what was now called the Cathcart Catwalk Challenge. I was proud of my citizenship class.

Trix had mentioned to me the idea of inviting a special guest of honour. It seemed an excellent idea – a good way of showing one of the school governors that today's teenagers are not all bad! I contacted the Reverend Patrick Cunningham, the local vicar who, in his younger days, had worked within the church in Kenya.

THE REV. PATRICK CUNNINGHAM

I was enormously encouraged that a group of Year 9 pupils were so engaged in the cause of alleviating world hunger. It was going to be a marvellous occasion and I much looked forward to it.

WIKI

The timing, I now see, was not great.

After exams, Cathcart goes weird. The sun is in the sky, work is over until the autumn, the holidays are still two weeks away. People are bored, restless.

But this year, there was the Cathcart Catwalk Challenge. The posters, with Kate Moss in a Cathcart tie and not much else, had sent out all the wrong messages. It was not Africa, nor giving to charity, that was on people's minds as they made their way to the school hall that night. It was having a blinding good time.

I was on the door, taking tickets. All the seats had been sold but, on the day, Trix had told me to let in people without tickets, as long as they paid at the door.

'Where will they sit?' I had asked.

'They'll fit in somehow,' she had said. Before I could say anything else, she came up with the usual killer argument. 'Each of those tickets will help feed a starving child.'

What could I say to that?

Ten minutes before the start of the show, it was a sell-out. And that was when a gang from the Lower Sixth – about eight boys and three girls – arrived. They were loud and some of them smelt of beer. They paid for a couple of tickets. Then, before I could collect the rest of the money, their ringleader, a loud, good-at-games type called Damien

Sinclair, pushed past me and, laughing, the others followed him.

By the time I got into the hall, they were sprawled around the catwalk in front of the seats. I looked for Trix or Holly but they were backstage, helping Jade with the 'models'. As I did my best to get some ticket money off the Lower Sixth gang, another five or six boys swaggered in. They actually laughed at the people who had bought tickets.

JADE

We should have had a couple of bouncers, like they have outside nightclubs. Instead we had Wiki Church, blinking at them. Terrific.

HOLLY

The hall looked good. I had managed to persuade Trix that filling the place with depressing photographs would spoil the atmosphere. So to make the point she wanted to get over, there was a table at the back of the hall with refreshments designed to reflect the theme of the evening.

Instead of soft drinks, there was water. For food, each member of the audience would be given a dish representing a day's food their money would be providing for an African child: one meatball and some unappetizing slop called mealie meal.

OK, it was gimmicky but at the time we thought it could work.

Miss Fothergill arrived with a priest in tow. He was dressed in full church gear, a tall, smiling man who wore glasses and a sincere, innocent expression on his face.

Miss Fothergill did an embarrassed flailing gesture in my direction. 'William, this is the Reverend Patrick Cunningham.' I shook his hand. It was like a sockful of cold porridge. 'William is one of this evening's organizers,' she explained.

'Well done, William,' said the vicar. 'You've done a marvellous job.'

I led them into the hall, up the central aisle to the two seats that had been reserved for them. Sinclair was sitting in one, a sleepy-looking Lower Sixth girl with tousled hair was in the other.

'Thank you, Damien,' said Miss Fothergill.

Grumbling, Sinclair and his girlfriend stood up and perched nearby on the edge of the stage.

By the time I got back to the door, more members of the Lower Sixth had made their way into the hall without tickets. The noise of chat and laughter was deafening.

Yup, there was no doubt about it. Trouble was in the air.

JADE

For the record, right? My bit of the show was just fine. The models were all there. A few looked kind of tragic, but most of them were OK.

A couple of minutes before the show as due to start, my friend Charlotte, who was dressed as a hippy, took a peek through the curtain.

'It's packed,' she whispered. 'Most of the Sixth are here.'

'I'm scared,' someone muttered.

'It'll be cool,' I said. 'Just think of Africa, right?'

We laughed. Possibly for the last time that evening.

WIKI

The lights went down. A spotlight hit the catwalk. The music came on, an old-fashioned big-band number from the beginning of time.

Someone said something at the back and there was laughter.

The girls came out one after another. Jade, who always fancied herself as a model, had suggested that the show should open with some really old clothes our grandparents used to wear way back in the last century.

It was a bad, bad idea. Any hope of the show being taken seriously drained away as girls strolled in wearing weird fancy-dress outfits. Soon they became aware that there were Lower Sixth people lounging on the floor near the catwalk looking up at them. They tried to joke it up, which encouraged more whoops and comments.

By the time Jade came on dressed in her best outfit, the evening had taken a serious dive for the worse. She strutted forward, a fixed smile on her face, but I could tell from the angry flush of colour on her cheeks, her narrowed eyes, the way she turned, that she was upset.

There were slightly mocking cheers as the lights went up at the end of the first half.

It had been Trix's idea that, after a tremendously successful thirty minutes of fashion on the catwalk, the audience would be ready to hear about starvation in Africa. Then the models would come out again, do one last twirl, and the audience would vote for the best costume – the winner of the Cathcart Catwalk Charity Challenge.

Big mistake.

HOLLY

Miss Fothergill had discovered a film about a place in Ethiopia where the children are hungry and rain never falls and the crops wither and everyone has really terrible diseases. She and Trix decided that it would make for a perfect good-citizen moment during the Catwalk Challenge. They downloaded it and borrowed the Film Society's big monitor.

There was a moment of silence as Trix introduced the film but when the voice-over, by a famous American actress, started, the restlessness in the audience soon returned.

'Did you know that three hundred million children go to bed hungry every night?' went the commentary.

'Yeah, I'm one of them,' said a voice at the back.

Someone tried to restore quiet, but there was more stifled laughter. No one was really watching the film any more.

I was sitting beside Trix. At first when I felt her body shaking, I thought she was crying. Then I realized she was trembling with anger.

I should have said something – stopped her getting back

on that stage – but by the time I realized she was about to make a bad situation a whole lot worse, it was too late.

WIKI

When she's angry, Trix can be a very scary sight but somehow, as she jumped up on the stage and stood in front of that screen, it was never going to work. It was Saturday night, summer term. She was too small, too pale, too serious.

'Thank you very much for reminding me just how *selfish* rich people can be,' were her opening words. Her voice sound strangled, well bred – even a bit silly.

There were sarcastic trills and ironic applause.

'What you're doing is actually laughing at starvation. How does that make you feel?'

'We're laughing at you, you div,' someone shouted. There was applause.

Trix was losing it. All the hurt that she felt on behalf of the children of Africa came flooding out, but her voice was shrill and what she said got lost in the noise. A few words and phrases – 'chronic disease', 'orphans', 'ravaged by disease', 'making a difference' – could just be heard above the chat and the laughter, but no one was listening any more.

MARK

Major confession. I was in the back row and, as things began to slide out of control, I leaned back in my seat and reached for one of the meatballs on the table behind my chair. I bounced it in my hand a few times. Then, half-jokingly, I pretended to throw it at the stage.

I swear I had no idea what was going to happen next.

HOLLY

Mark Bliss started it. I noticed him tossing this ball up and down in his hand, as if he were playing cricket or something. Then I realized it was a meatball.

MARK

A couple of guys from the Lower Sixth in front of me noticed what I was doing. 'Where did you get that?' one of them whispered. I nodded in the direction of the table. As Trix Johansson-Bell droned on about death and disaster, they scuttled out of their seats and grabbed a handful of meatballs each.

HOLLY

Who threw the first meatball? Who cares?

All I know is that others were quick to follow. One meatball flew through the air, then another. Someone in the audience said, 'Food fight!' There was laughter and a general move towards the food table.

I still think the moment might have passed, if Jade hadn't become involved.

JADE

The models were standing to the side of the stage when food started flying. I thought, excuse me, Jade Hart does not appear on stage in her best Karen Millen dress to have some Neanderthal dorks throw bits of meat at her. One of the ball things hit me on the shoulder, leaving a nasty greasy mark.

I did what any girl would do. I picked it up and threw it back as hard as I could. So sue me.

MISS FOTHERGILL

I simply could not believe what was happening. I'm all for high spirits but the older pupils were taking advantage of the situation. When the models started throwing food back at the audience, Trix stopped talking and stared around her in amazement.

'I'm terribly sorry about this,' I said to Patrick Cunningham.

To my surprise, he patted my hand. 'I'm used to it,' he said. 'I deal quite a lot with delinquent teenagers.'

HOLLY

I had an idea. If the film stopped and the models did their last walk before the actual Catwalk Challenge – the vote – people would settle down. I couldn't stop the film but I switched on the music, a hip-hop thing that Jade had chosen.

WIKI

Now there really was confusion. The film was still running but the commentary couldn't be heard above the sound of the music. Some of the models began doing their last walk up and down the catwalk. Others – take a bow, Jade Hart – continued with the food fight. Trix just stood there in the centre of the stage, looking wide-eyed and horrified.

It was at that moment that the guest of honour in the front row decided to take control of the situation. The Rev. Patrick Cunningham stood up, hopped on the stage and, with a big friendly smile, held up both arms.

'Kids, kids –' he said. 'Perhaps at this point, I may –'

Whack! A meatball caught him square in the eye. It must have been quite a well-cooked one because he staggered back and said a word that I never thought I would hear spoken by a vicar.

At that very moment, there was a crash from the back of the room as the double doors to the hall flew open.

HOLLY

There, like an avenging fury, stood the headmaster, Mr Griffiths.

Everything stopped – the cheering, the food-throwing, the laughter – but the music played on, deafeningly.

In my panic, it took me about thirty seconds to switch it off.

When the Head spoke, his voice was quiet and scary.

'Would someone mind telling me what is going on here?'

26

Miss Fothergill stood up.

'As you know, Head, this is a show . . . er, in aid of Africa – the starving. Children.' She hesitated. 'Er, and the Reverend Cunningham is here as guest of honour, which is nice,' she added, as if that somehow made everything all right.

On stage, the vicar wiped some meatball grease from his eye. 'Hello, Nigel,' he said uncertainly.

Mr Griffiths seemed about to say something, then thought better of it. He looked around the room.

'Starving children in Africa, is it?' he said in an ice-cold voice. 'It looks more like a *rave* to me. Who is responsible for this?'

There was a moment's silence. Then Trix stepped forward.

'I am, sir,' she said.

'You?'

The Head glared at her as if no words could express his disgust and disappointment. He looked around. The silence stretched over seconds. Somebody had to speak. It had been Trix's big project but she shouldn't take the rap for all of us. I waited for Holly or Jade to speak up. Both were staring at the floor. I took a deep breath.

'And me,' I said.

Now that he had two victims, Griffo looked as if he had seen enough. 'No one leaves the hall until it is tidied up and returned to its normal state,' he said briskly. 'When Miss Fothergill gives you permission, you will return to your respective houses and remain there for the rest of the evening. And you two – Church and Johansson-Bell

– I'll need to see you in my study at nine thirty tomorrow morning.'

He left, gently closing the doors behind him. The Cathcart Catwalk Charity Challenge was over.

V Day - 16

WIKI

At Cathcart there are no such things as second thoughts. You are right or you are wrong.

Even Trix, who will continue to argue about things when everyone else has fallen asleep or is rolling around with their hands over their ears screaming for mercy, knew that there was no point in explaining to the head teacher that the great fashion-show disaster was not caused by us.

The following morning we went to the Griffon's lair. Anyone who has ever been in trouble at school will know the sort of stuff that followed. Irresponsible, blah . . . utterly inappropriate behaviour, blah . . . bad example blah . . . given an inch, took a yard, blah . . . let everyone down, especially yourselves, blah blah blah blah.

End result : we were given Uniform Rustication (Cathcart language for having to stay in college and wear your school uniform at all times) for the last two weeks of the summer term. Oh, and our parents would be informed.

MRS GLORIA CHURCH

I cannot lie – it was a shock when we received a call from Mr Griffiths that day.

William had been in trouble, he said. There had been

29

an incident of serious disruption. He had decided to make allowances because of William's 'circumstances' (he is one of the few children of colour in his year), but there would be disciplinary action – 'Uniform Rustication', he called it – until the end of the summer term.

William disruptive? Frankly, the idea beggared belief. He has always been the apple of our eye. When he won a scholarship to the famous Cathcart College, we were the proudest parents in the world. It was tough for us financially – even though his fees were paid by the school, there were books and clothes to buy – but until now we had believed that we were doing the right thing. Our only child was going to have chances in his life that his father and I had never had.

Now we were very worried. If he was guilty of serious disruption at fourteen, what would he be like at seventeen? That night, his father rang him. They had a very, very serious talk.

EVA JOHANSSON

I believe I received a message from the au pair that someone had rung from the school but I was preparing to go to Hollywood to pitch for a film project at the time and let it ride. Trix has always been good at looking after herself.

JADE

Don't get me wrong, but I do think Trix had to take some responsibility for what happened.

Maybe Holly and I should have owned up to the Griffon but here's the way I saw it: as the leading model, I had made the biggest sacrifice for her precious African village. I was the person who was laughed at, who was made to feel stupid. It was *my* Karen Millen dress that got stained when things started going downhill. I had been punished already.

You know what? She never actually said sorry. All she went on about was how the evening had made only thirty-eight pounds. I admit it's not much, given that we were totally humiliated, but Holly and I agreed on one thing. It was time to move on. Those African kids had thirty-eight pounds more than they would have had if we had not taken the trouble to put on our designer clothes. Trix was our best friend and all that but she should have had the decency not to mention that village in Africa for a few days.

Instead, on and on she went.

And get this. She went on seeing Wiki. They were suddenly buddies – nothing more, thank goodness, that would be full-on weird. But Trix and Wiki Church? It was a strange one, no doubt about it.

Two days after the great catwalk disaster, we saw them chatting away at lunch. As we watched them from across

31

the dining hall, Holly pointed out that we were now best friends with someone who was best friends with Wiki Church, which made us virtually best friends with Wiki Church ourselves.

A serious reputation crisis was looming.

HOLLY

She strode about the school in her uniform, making everyone feel guilty. Nothing at Cathcart is ever fair but, even by the school's low standards of justice, it was tough that the one person (two, if you include Wiki) who had wanted to do good was punished because a group of sad boys felt the need to show off.

I should have said something in the hall. I was going to, but suddenly the Head was gone and somehow I had said nothing. Neither Trix nor Wiki ever made a fuss about the fact that Jade and I had kept our heads down, but it's fair to say that for a few days we didn't feel great about ourselves.

V Day – 13

WIKI

Trix was in a bad way. It takes a lot to knock her off track but, during the days that followed that weekend, she became really withdrawn. It was as if she felt that she had personally failed the children in that village in Mali.

At first, Holly and Jade tried to cheer her up and talk about the holidays but I think Trix wanted to stay angry. That was why she spent more time with me. I let her talk about the African village, which now totally obsessed her.

She told me she had to make things right. It was almost as if she saw the world divided into Cathcart College and Africa. We had a choice – to go one way or the other.

Africa had taken a hit from Cathcart. Now she wanted revenge.

MISS FOTHERGILL

I was in something of a quandary. I am not a rich person and there was quite a serious possibility that, after the fashion show, I would be, as the Head put it, 'relieved of my position'.

Of course, I was concerned about Trix. I had her in for tea several times during those last two weeks of term and we discussed how best to make things better after recent disappointments.

'Use your anger, Trix,' I used to say. 'Channel it into your work next year. Being miserable doesn't help anyone.'

Sadly, she was no longer listening to me. She was polite enough, but sometimes I caught her looking at me in a way that was almost judgemental. It was as if I had failed some sort of test.

EVA JOHANSSON

Trix rang several times towards the end of that term. Something about Africa, was it? A fashion show that had gone wrong?

I like to be there for my daughter but, when it comes to these little teen crises, my attitude is simple: that was why I sent her to Cathcart College. Boarding schools are good at dealing with children. I'm hopeless when it comes to discipline – too nice for my own good, Jason says.

Between you and me, I would have preferred her to be at a day school but, for her sake, I thought a boarding school would be a good thing. After I had divorced her father, the Drunk (he doesn't have a name as far as I am concerned), I had moved in with Jason Everleigh, the well-known sports agent.

I'll be honest. Jason and Trix were chalk and cheese. Jase is a successful and good-looking person who appreciates the importance of earning a decent living. Trix looks fine (she's my daughter, I would say that!) but it's no secret that she'll never be a model or an actress. Plus, she has inherited her father's attitude to authority. I like spirit but Trix is not just independent-minded and feisty, as a young girl should be. She is a rebel. Quite often, in the early days of my marriage to Jason, she would talk to our friends about the most unsuitable things – how children are dying of AIDS in Africa and all that.

Now, if you're out for a nice dinner party with a well-known actress and her millionaire husband, you don't want some funny little thing sitting at the table talking about death and disgusting diseases. It's not polite and it's not nice.

So this is what Jason said one night: 'That child needs space and we need space. Boarding school is the answer.'

The Drunk objected, of course. Trix was not crazy about the idea either. But sometimes one has to be firm as a parent.

With Trix's little crisis that term, Jase and I agreed that we had made the right decision. The best place for her was among people who knew how to handle these things. It's called tough love.

WIKI

Trix became weirdly interested in the case of a disappearing girl.

The child's name was Michaela Parry.

I don't read the newspapers much but you had to be deaf, dumb and blind not to have heard of Michaela. She was seven, the daughter of a couple who lived near London. During the Easter holiday, she had been playing in the garden of the family house while the Polish au pair was bathing her baby sister inside.

Michaela disappeared. One moment she was there,

the next she was gone.

The papers went mad. It was like this great detective story only it was real. Some blamed the parents for putting their jobs before their family. Others thought the Polish au pair was a bit dodgy. There were stories about Mrs Parry's first marriage, sightings from around the world.

Of course, it was all very sad, but I couldn't quite see why Trix had suddenly become so obsessed about the case of a child she had never even met.

It was one afternoon, a week after exams had finished, when I began to understand what was going on.

I was in Trix's room, chatting, keeping her company, when she pulled this cardboard box from under her bed. She turned it upside down on her bed. Newspaper cuttings tumbled out. Every one of them was about the case of Michaela Parry.

She riffled through them angrily. 'Its obscene,' she said quietly.

'Yeah.' I decided to humour her. Trix in this strange mood could go ballistic at the slightest excuse. 'Who do you think did it?'

She looked at me, surprised. 'I don't care,' she said.

'But—'

'Don't you see? That's not the point.' She began searching through the cuttings, then handed me the front page of an evening newspaper. The headline read, 'MICHAELA STILL ALIVE, SAY POLICE.'

'Look at the bottom of the page.' Trix stabbed the paper with a finger. There was a small additional story.

RESCUE FUND CLIMBS HIGHER

The plight of little Michaela Parry has touched people across Europe and America, it was revealed yesterday. The Find Michaela fund has now reached a staggering £600,000, thanks to generous donations by supporters across the world. One donation, by a city businessman who wished to remain anonymous, was for £100,000. 'The Parrys are deeply touched by the help they are getting,' a family spokesman said. 'Every penny improves the chance of reuniting Michaela with her family.'

Do you want to help find little Michaela? Make your donation online at findmichaelaparry.com.

'Obscene,' Trix repeated.

I was confused. 'Isn't it a good thing that people want to help?' I asked.

She looked at me as if I were completely mad.

'Think about it, Wiki,' she said. 'A child in Africa dies from hunger every five seconds. No one even thinks about it. There's nothing in the papers. When we tried to raise money for dying children, it was like this big joke. But when one little white girl goes missing, it's a big international story. The whole country has a nervous breakdown.'

'It's a bit nearer home, I suppose.'

'Six hundred thousand pounds, Wiki. Have you any idea how many African children that could save? It costs UNICEF seventeen dollars to inoculate a child against the six major diseases – to save their lives. So think how many lives could be saved with six hundred thousand pounds.'

I did the calculation. 'Nearly fifty-four thousand,' I said.

'Exactly,' she said with a slightly surprised look in my direction. 'But just because their parents don't have a nice job and a big house, no one cares.'

I began to see what she was on about.

'To be fair, people are giving money out of kindness,' I said. 'It's just that their kindness is a bit blind. They don't see things the way that you do.'

Trix was staring into the distance. 'Well, maybe they should be shown how to,' she said grimly.

'Of course they should,' I said quickly. Then, more to head off another lecture than anything else, I murmured, 'If only there were a way we could use that Michaela Parry type of generosity to help the right people.'

'How do you mean, Wik?'

'If only we could show people that it's not just children from their own little world who need help.'

'Like some kind of demonstration, you mean?' Trix was looking at me with a worrying intensity. 'Turn people's generosity around?'

'Yeah,' I said. 'Well, sort of.'

She looked down at the newspaper cutting. 'You're right,' she said quietly. 'Wiki Church, you are a genius.'

Then she did something truly scary. She hugged me. 'Thank you,' she whispered in my ear. 'Thank you so much.'

I was just about to ask her what she was thanking me for when the door opened.

JADE

Ugh, please.

Holly and I walked into Trix's room and she was in this

38

clinch with, of all people, Wiki Church. It was the most disgusting thing I have ever seen – ever.

HOLLY

'Oh,' I said, trying to be cool about the whole thing. 'Is this a bad moment?'

Wiki leaped back as if someone had given him an electric shock. His glasses had misted up and his chin was going up and down like he was a goldfish that had just been taken out of its bowl.

'It's a very good moment,' said Trix.

'Are you really, really sure about that?' said Jade, who can always be relied upon to say the wrong thing. 'I mean, Wiki? Not being funny but, Trix, maybe you should see a doctor or something.'

Trix stood up. 'Let's go out for a walk,' she said. 'Wiki has just had the most brilliant idea in the history of the world.'

WIKI

I had? Just what was my brilliant idea?

Trix crammed the newspaper cuttings back into the box and put it under her arm. Without another word, she walked out of the door.

Holly, Jade and I followed.

JADE

Picture it. Trix was marching ahead of us, carrying this cardboard box. Holly and I were tagging along out of curiosity. Speccy Boy was there too, still looking as if someone had just hit him on the head with a plank.

Trix headed for the park, a bit of woodland which is part of the grounds where Cathcartians are meant to look at the birds and the trees and do the whole joy-of-nature thing.

She knows what she's doing but the rest of us – even, I swear, Wiki Church – have one thought on our minds.

It goes: Uhhhnnn? What the – ????

WIKI

The four of us were walking down this path between two rows of rhododendron bushes when we saw Mark Bliss and his friend Tom Parkinson coming towards us.

Trix walked straight up to them. 'Lighter,' she said.

Mark and Tom looked confused for a moment. Then Mark (a well-known smoker) reached into his pocket.

'Cheers.' Trix took the lighter and brushed past the boys.

'Hang on,' Mark called out, but Trix was on her way.

'What's up with her?' he asked but, because none of us knew the answer to the question, we walked past trying to look as if we knew what was going on.

Deep into the park, Trix led us into this clearing. She put the box down, crouched beside it and set fire to the newspapers. Soon there was a nice blaze going.

We four stood watching it for a moment.

'What exactly was this great plan?' Holly asked.

Trix's face was more alive and happy than it had been for weeks. She looked up at us, the flames reflected in her sparkling eyes.

'We're going to commit a crime,' she said.

MARK

Hey, I needed that lighter.

At least, that was what I told Tom a few moments after Little Miss Save-the-World mugged me for my lighter in the park.

The truth was that I sensed that something interestingly freaky was coming down with those three girls and Church. So I doubled back on my own and followed them.

When I found them, they were standing around this little fire. Trix was talking and whatever she was saying was so interesting that I was able to sneak up on them and hunker down behind a bush.

JADE

There's only one thing scarier than Trix when she's angry and that's Trix when she's happy. A weird grin settles on her face. Her eyes sparkle as if, at any moment, she's going to break down and cry with excitement. She's like some religious wacko who thinks she's seen a miracle and wants to tell the world about it.

'Er, crime?' This was me. 'Any danger of your being a tad more specific?'

'It's simple,' she said. 'One day there's this fourteen-year-old girl at the start of her holidays. The next day there isn't. She vanishes. Because –' She paused like someone about to give the punchline to a joke – 'she's been kidnapped.'

HOLLY

'Kidnapped?!'

The word came blurting out of my mouth more loudly than I had intended.

Trix put her hand to her lips.

'What exactly are we talking about here?' I whispered. 'You're speaking in riddles, Trix.'

'OK, so here's the broad outline,' she said. 'You guys kidnap me. There's this big fuss when it's discovered I'm missing – daughter of famous actress, yaddah yaddah. Money is raised to find me. At a certain point, the kidnappers – that's you – say you'll release the victim – that's me – if the money is sent to Africa.'

'Broad outline is right,' Wiki muttered.

Jade gave a panicky little laugh. 'You have some serious issues, dude,' she said.

Trix held up a hand. 'So now we get down to the details,' she said.

MARK

I listened. At first I thought that Trix was telling some sort of story but that was hardly her style. Someone said the word 'kidnap'. As they huddled together, I looked at the faces of Jade, Holly and Wiki.

This was no story. Whatever that little gang was planning, it was for real.

WIKI

We were now in the dying days of the summer term, a downward spiral of true madness. People got drunk, fell in love, played tricks on teachers.

Just briefly, it seemed as if Trix's plan was another bit of end-of-year wildness. I thought that by the time the holidays rolled around, our conversation in the park would be no more than an embarrassing memory.

But something worrying happened over the days following our meeting in the park. Trix seemed to be taking it seriously. At every possible opportunity, she would take me aside to discuss how the plot would work. She lost interest in lessons. The only people she talked to were Holly, Jade and me.

Her face changed. It was as if the sun had come out in her life at last – as if she had a reason to live. She was scarily happy.

People talk about 'Living the dream'. Trix could do more than live the dream. She made other people believe it. Gradually, the craziest scheme in the history of crazy schemes began to seem almost possible.

Not that it was all talk. Trix quickly moved into action, cancelling the holiday she had planned to spend with Holly and Jade in Italy. Then she enrolled at some kind of summer camp – a summer camp that she would never see.

Her mother and stepfather just nodded this through.

EVA JOHANSSON

Towards the end of term, while I was in Los Angeles, I received a slightly odd call from my daughter. She told me that she had changed her mind about the summer holidays.

All right, I shall put my cards on the table now. I was not thrilled. I had agreed with Jason that I would come back to England at the end of July to see Trix off to the villa Holly's family had rented in Italy. Then I would return to LA.

It is possible that I told Trix that no way was I going to change these plans.

She informed me that was not a problem. She had decided to go to a summer camp instead. She had other friends there, she said. It was just a question of my paying the fees.

I agreed, of course. It was expensive, sure, but if my daughter was looked after while I was in America, no price was too high. We have always been quite a generous family.

WIKI

Then Trix started on me. What were my plans for the summer holidays? Had my family booked their air tickets to somewhere warm?

I told her that my parents didn't need to buy air tickets

to where we were going – a week's camping holiday in Cornwall.

She looked surprised. In her world, everyone went abroad in August. Then she cheered up.

'That's great,' she said. 'It'll be easy to cancel, right?'

I made the call.

MRS GLORIA CHURCH

When William rang towards the end of the summer term to say that he would be staying with his new friend Trix Johansson-Bell for the first part of the holidays, we were naturally disappointed. At the same time we were glad that at last he was making friends among his peers.

He works hard, our William, and we knew it was not easy for him settling in at a smart private school. After the disappointment of the Uniform Rustication, we believed that he was doing something to put his life in order.

WIKI

Like a general planning her campaign, Trix turned her attention to Jade and Holly.

JADE

My #!!?*$%!* vacation!

When Trix said, 'Well, the first thing we've got to do is blank Italy,' I freaked.

I had been looking forward to that vacation for months! Trix and I had been going to stay with Holly's parents at their totally awesome villa with a swimming pool and a media room and a veranda and loads of Italian servants. Now suddenly Trix was out of the picture.

HOLLY

That was just the start. Trix's next idea was that a few days after what she now called 'The Vanish', Jade and I would fly back to England, too upset to enjoy our holiday. Then after 'V Day', the 'gang' (I promise you she was talking like this) would gather for the next phase.

I'll admit it. We humoured her. There were so many holes in the little boat that Trix was trying to sail that it was obviously never even going to get out of the harbour.

It was a shame that she wasn't going to be in Italy, but, between you and me, all that save-the-world stuff was beginning to get on our nerves.

There's a time and a place for worrying about kids dying in Africa and summer holidays lying by a pool in Tuscany isn't it.

Sure, Trix. We'll go with the whole self-kidnap thing. That's what friends are for. We won't even talk about it when everything goes belly up. As it surely will.

Won't it?

V Day - 8

WIKI

From the start, Trix was determined that no adults were going to be involved but it began to look as if not even she was going to get away with that. Er, transport? Er, maybe even a house for us to stay in?

The first candidate was Trix's real father, Peter Bell. He was some kind of journalist who had fallen on hard times. He sounded wild enough to go along with the kidnap idea but he turned out to have one serious disadvantage. He was always drunk.

I was no use, because my parents and their friends are about the most law-abiding people you could ever meet.

Then Jade's two brothers were briefly in the frame.

JADE

I don't talk about my brothers. It's complicated. Understand this if nothing else about my two big bros: the less you know about them, the better it is for you. The situation's mega complicated.

That's kind of what I told Trix.

MARK

It was bugging me. I don't like mysteries. I noticed that the four of them – Trix, Holly, Jade and Wiki Church – were spending more time together. They ate lunch at the same table, hung out in each other's rooms. One day I heard mention of something called 'V Day'. What on earth was that all about? Some kind of girlie Valentine's Day thing? I wasn't jealous or anything but I was kind of interested. If there was an adventure coming down the track, I wanted to jump on it.

I decided to push a bit to see what happened.

One lunch I noticed Church in the dining-room queue. I took my place behind him.

'All right, Willie?' I said.

'I prefer William,' he said, blinking in that annoying way of his.

'Off to see your girlfriends, are you?'

He looked away, saying nothing.

'Who's your favourite? Jade's a bit tall for you, I'd say.'

'They're just friends,' he muttered, blink-blink, sniff-sniff.

'What?' I said. 'Like a little gang, are you? A posse?'

He had reached the front of the queue and was helping himself to food.

'The trouble with gangs is that you've got to have secrets, isn't it, Willie?'

'William.'

'If you're planning a – well, say for the sake of argument, a kidnap, it's really important that no one else knows about it.'

I had his attention now. He even forgot to blink for a couple of seconds.

'What are you talking about?' he said.

I winked. 'I think you know what I'm talking about.'

He moved away so fast that his plate was only half full.

'You forgot your potatoes, Willie,' I called after him.

HOLLY

Wiki came back to the table. He looked as if he was about to puke.

He sat down without a word and, staring down at his plate, he said, 'Mark Bliss knows about The Vanish. Someone must have told him.'

I looked up and Bliss was watching us. He was sitting alone at a table on the far side of the dining room. He put a finger to his lips and smiled.

As in: *Shh.*

WIKI

I had a bit of a problem with Mark Bliss. The problem was that I hated him.

He had the Cathcart look, the Cathcart face, the Cathcart walk, the Cathcart hairstyle, the Cathcart drawl. He played cricket. He had a lot of friends. Some of the girls (the airheads, admittedly) actually thought he was cool.

Mark made everything look easy. He was born to go to Cathcart. You could see his future in his face, the way he moved through the world. Respectable exam results would lead to a posh university and then a job in big business. Even at fourteen, Mark was on his way.

So when we discovered that somehow or other Mark knew of our plan, three of us assumed that the jig was up before we had even started.

The odd one out was Trix.

MARK

I was primed. I was ready to have some serious fun.

But moments after Church had passed on the news that their little plan was just about to become the best joke of that week, something surprising happened.

Trix Johansson-Bell, the mad fashion-show organizer, stood up and headed in my direction.

This, I thought, could be interesting.

She sat down and put her sharp little elbows on my table. Then she smiled.

Whoa. It was a surprise, that smile. It kind of disarmed me, to tell the truth.

'Hey, Mark,' she said.

'How you going?' I said, a bit uneasily.

'So.' The smile was even brighter. 'Who was it who told you?'

I shrugged and said nothing.

'It has to be Holly or Jade. It wasn't Wiki and it wasn't me. No one else knows.'

I glanced across at the two girls in question. They were not my favourite people in the year. The American Jade thought she was some kind of teen beauty queen, and Holly behaved like she knew the answer to life. The idea that either of them might be a friend was a serious rep-buster.

'What makes you think someone told me?' I said. 'They didn't, as it happens.'

Trix frowned. I could tell that she was going to get the truth out of me somehow.

'Have you still got my lighter?' I asked. 'You've had your little bonfire after all.'

'You followed us.'

'I wanted my lighter.'

'You heard everything we said.'

It was my turn to smile. 'Yep.'

'Were you alone?'

'I was.'

'What about Parkinson?'

'I told you. I was alone.'

'Have you told anyone else?'

I laughed. 'Why on earth would I want to talk about a bunch of weirdos talking about a plan that is totally and utterly demented?'

'You promise?'

'I promise.'

Trix drummed the table with the fingers of her left hand. She seemed to reach a decision.

'We need one more person.'

'What?'

'Yes,' she said, almost talking to herself. 'This is very, very good. It could work out perfectly. You'd be a great member of the team.'

'Trix, forget it. I don't even like "the team". I mean, why should I help you? People get into trouble for this kind of thing.'

'No,' she said. 'This kind of thing is what can save lives, Mark – thousands of children's lives in Africa. You saw what happened at the fashion show. You were part of it. People don't care – and we've got to make them care.'

'You don't get it, do you? I don't care about caring. Strange as it may sound to you, I've kind of reached the conclusion that Africa is NMP – not my problem.'

'That's the real Mark Bliss speaking, is it?' The disappointment in her voice got to me in a way I couldn't quite understand at the time.

'I don't see anybody else around.'

'Because I heard that Mark Bliss was up for anything.' She gave me the look again, straight in the eyes. 'That's what I heard, Mark.'

Then she added in a matter-of-fact tone, 'What are your plans for the summer holidays?'

'I'm going away with my family at the end of the holidays for a couple of weeks.'

'Great.' She stood up. 'I'll be in touch.'

'Trix,' I said, 'I haven't agreed to anything.'

The sunny smile was back. She reached into her pocket and chucked my lighter on to the table. Then – this I could not believe – she actually winked at me. She stood there for a moment, as if expecting me to say something else.

'All right,' I said, just to get rid of her. 'I'll think about it.'

She laughed. 'You already have,' she said.

WIKI

I felt sick. When Trix came sauntering back to the table, I was wondering how she had managed to get Bliss to agree to keep a secret. It occurred to me that – even better – she

53

had discovered that he had no real clue as to what was going on.

But no.

She sat down, looked around the table and said these fateful words: 'He's in.'

'What?' After a stunned few seconds, I managed to speak. 'Who's in?'

'Mark Bliss. He followed us in the park and heard the plan. He's perfect.' Trix actually seemed surprised that we seemed so shocked. 'No one will suspect him and he'll have contacts.'

'But . . . but . . .' Unusually, Jade seemed lost for words.

'But what?' asked Trix.

'But . . . *he's Mark Bliss*!' Jade blurted out.

An irritating smile had settled on Trix's face. 'Mark's not as bad as he likes to make out.'

'And he agreed?' Holly asked.

'Virtually,' said Trix. 'He was kind of iffy to start with. But he'll come round. Trust me.'

HOLLY

Trust her? She had to be out of her tiny mind. If you lined up all the people in the Remove who are unreliable, unlikely to help others, un-almost anything you care to mention, standing at the front of the queue, smirking, a lock of hair covering one eye, hands in pockets, would be Mark Bliss.

We told her all this. We reminded her that it had been Mark 'Mr Cool' Bliss who had started the food fight at the fashion show. We invited her to look at his stupid face as he grinned at us from across the room.

Waste of breath.

JADE

It was official. Trix was seriously nuts. I should have pulled out there and then.

But it was all becoming so out-of-this-world strange that I was kind of keen on sticking around to see what would happen next.

Innocent curiosity. That was what did for me in the end.

HOLLY

Five minutes into the madness and I had heard quite enough. I told her she was out of her tiny mind to think that I would do anything – like, *anything* – with Mark Bliss, and left them there at the table.

I waited for Jade at the door. It took five seconds for her to push back her chair and storm off too.

'I'm so out of this,' she said as she swept past me.

'Me too,' I said, following her. 'Let's leave it to Trix, Wiki and Mark – the dream team.'

We both laughed.

MARK

Mark Bliss is not a natural joiner of gangs – particularly when the gang has got girls and a nerdy black kid as its other members. If Mark Bliss wants to do charity, he does it by giving coins to a dosser in the street.

It's just the way I am.

So I was kind of surprised to find that I started doing what Trix Johansson-Bell had asked me to do. I did think about it. I began to see ways that it – The Vanish or whatever we were calling it – might work.

I even began to think of the people I'd have to deal with – a girl suffering from a bad attack of idealism, a geek with glasses, a bouncy lacrosse type and a very stupid American beanpole – as a sort of gang.

Maybe Trix had some kind of African hoodoo on her side, because suddenly Mark Bliss was interested.

MISS FOTHERGILL

Teenage girls are surprisingly resilient. Life can deal them the most fearsome knocks, but they pick themselves up and are soon back to their old selves.

As the end of term approached, the smile was back on Trix's face. She seemed to have found some new friends

56

– little William Church and Mark Bliss, neither of whom seemed quite her type.

She seemed less interested in her citizenship lessons, even when we were talking about problems in the Third World.

After one lesson, as the rest of the class were leaving, I mentioned that I had been surprised that she had had so little to say about a subject that had once meant so much to her.

She gave me an odd little smile which, when I thought about it later, seemed somehow less friendly than I might have wished.

'I guess I've moved on,' she said. 'I've decided that direct action is the thing.'

Direct action? At the time I *did* wonder vaguely what she was talking about.

MARK

I still don't know how it happened but somehow, without my even agreeing, I was in. The Trixter, as I now called her, has the kind of willpower that's like a supernatural force.

The day after our meeting in the canteen, I called by her house. When I knocked on the door and breezed in, she was sitting at her desk. She glanced over her shoulder, as if she was expecting to see me.

I slumped down on the bed and looked around. Staring at me from every wall were the big dark eyes of starving African kids.

'Hey, cool posters,' I said.

'Yes.' She wrote something on the pad in front of her. 'I like them.'

'So this is what it's all for, The Vanish?'

She held up her hand. In all Cathcart houses, there is no such thing as privacy. The rooms are cubicles with thin board walls.

'I wasn't going to say anything,' I said in a low voice. 'I'm not stupid, you know.'

'I know you're not.' She put down her pen. 'Let's go for a walk.'

She's a fast walker, the Trixter. At the time, as she strode around the cricket pitch like someone who's late for a bus, I thought she was playing me some kind of mind game, forcing me to keep up with her. For a while, I walked at my pace, hoping that, like any normal person, she would slow down.

Not the Trixter. If anything, she sped up. I actually had to run to catch up with her.

She told me, striding along, how the plan was going to work. She said that it was all that she thought about. She was going to prove to the world that being kind was not just a question of looking after people like yourself.

'Why now?' I asked, tagging along behind her like some kind of dog. 'Why not wait until you're older?'

'The whole point is that we're fourteen,' she said. 'We can change things. It's our world. It's our future. They think we're just kids, so we'll show them. This is what kids can do.'

Then she stopped, as if something had just occurred to her. 'We need a car and somewhere to stay.'

'Yeah, right.' I laughed. 'Easy-peasy.'

'Our hideout has got to be out of the way – no near

58

neighbours. All we need is someone who'll let us do what we want.'

She was off again, walking like a wind-up doll with a turbo engine.

'You'll know an adult like that,' she said. 'I just know it.'

There was something about the Trixter, I was discovering, that made you want to help her. She was so certain that anything seemed possible.

'I only know one person who lives really out of the way,' I called after her, 'and that's my godfather.'

She stopped, turned. 'Does he drive?'

'Sort of. He's got this old London taxi.'

'Tell me about him,' she said.

At least I had managed to slow Trix down for a moment. Walking at my pace, I told her a bit about Gideon Burrowes.

'He was my father's best friend at school – really intelligent but apparently a bit wiggy even then. He went to university to train to be a genius scientist. I've seen him skipping through books on nuclear physics like we would read a comic.'

'I don't read comics.'

'But then he went strange. At some point in his twenties, he gave up being a genius and went to live in Wales up in the mountains, all alone except for loads of cats. He makes rocking chairs.'

Trix walked in silence for a while.

'He sounds OK,' she said eventually. 'There's nothing weird about liking cats or making rocking chairs.'

'He doesn't have a TV or read the papers. He cuts his own hair. He's convinced that the government are spying on him.'

'Maybe they are.'

'He won't have fillings put in his teeth because he thinks they contain receptors which can read what he's thinking. He refuses to fill out forms. He's had fake number plates put on this old taxi that he drives so that the authorities will never know where he is.'

'Ah.' Trix frowned. 'I must admit he does sound a bit strange.'

'My dad says that, in his way, Gideon's the sanest person he has ever known.'

GODFATHER GIDEON BURROWES

Wear dark glasses, Mark said. I liked that. It intrigued me. As if we were playing a game. Perhaps we were. He explained what he wanted me to do. I simply agreed. I made the list and agreed.

Get the taxi.

Drive to London.

Pick up Mark and a friend.

Pick up another friend on the way out.

Drive home.

Oh, and wear dark glasses.

Why ask questions? We are each individuals, a complex mass of molecules, prions, sinew and tissue. We were born with free will. It is our nature to create our own personal destiny not that of others.

Hence, a few basic ground rules to which I have more or less adhered since the age of nineteen.

Ask no questions of others.

If they ask questions of you, answer only those that give nothing away.

Privacy is the most important thing in the world.

No marriage, no love stuff. When I was young, one or two young ladies were misguided enough to take an interest in me. I managed to shake them off, thank heavens.

These days, I live on my own and rarely meet other people.

I have a telephone but I avoid answering it. I prefer to store messages upon an answering machine. Now and then, as in the case of my godson, there are people to whom I would like to speak. On those occasions, I return their call.

Something else I learned at nineteen. I don't like human beings much. If I have to see them at all, I prefer the small versions, the children. They take up less space in the world for a start.

My godson is all right – better than most humans, not as good as a cat – and he comes to stay with me once a year.

I have never known precisely what a godfather is supposed to do, so I take him shooting on my land, talk to him about science, generally let him breathe the air of freedom.

But it was a surprise when he rang me that July. Bringing pals, was he? I'd just have to put up with that.

Wear dark glasses, the boy said. I wasn't even sure I had a pair.

EVA JOHANSSON

I left Jason in LA, put my film project on hold for a week, and returned to England to send Trix to her summer camp. What would you expect? I am a mother. It's what mothers do.

My elder daughter is a strong character like me and was old enough to decide how she wished to spend her holidays. My job was to spend two days with Trix in England, put her on the train to her camp, and catch a flight back to LA.

I considered telling the Drunk that his daughter had changed her plans but I was on a busy-busy timeline at that moment. We had agreed that he would be seeing her for two weeks at the end of the holidays and that had not changed – or so I thought.

Besides, he probably would have been too off his face to understand.

PETE BELL

A call would have been good. Just a call. I may not be a candidate for Dad of the Year but she is my daughter.

But then my ex doesn't do nice. And Trix must have had something else on her mind. Maybe she was too busy saving the world to worry about her old dad.

V Day – 4

WIKI

On the last day of term – a hot, swimming-pool day – we met in the park, standing around a bench, trying not to look shifty.

Trix, who had somehow become our leader without anyone agreeing to it, went through the plan. Because the plan hardly existed, it didn't take long.

On the first day of the holidays, we would each go home. Holly and Jade would fly off to Italy with the de Vriess family.

On the third day of the holidays, I would meet Mark at his house in Chiswick. We would be collected in a taxi by his godfather, a Mr Burrowes, We would drive to Paddington Station, where, on a road called Praed Street, Trix would be waiting to be kidnapped.

We would kidnap her, drive out of London to Wales, where Mr Burrowes lives. After a couple of days, Holly and Jade would fly back to join us and then . . .

For the briefest moment, Trix lost her air of certainty as the plan came to an end.

'And then we decide on our next move,' she said.

'Excuse me, O mighty leader,' said Holly, trying to keep a straight face. 'But isn't that plan just the teensiest bit vague?'

Trix gave Holly a hard-eyed look and then eyeballed the rest of us for a moment.

64

'This can work,' she said quietly. 'This is going to save lives.'

JADE

Oh yeah, right. Like we really believed that.

V Day

WIKI

The day of The Vanish was to be like any other day. That was what we had agreed.

I got up early that morning, said goodbye to my parents, and took the bus to the station. I would be at Mark's house before ten.

HOLLY

It was not true that we forgot all about Trix, V Day and all that, but by the time it was due to take place we were in Italy, snoozing, sunbathing, lolling around in the pool now and then. We had other things on our minds.

JADE

A holiday vibe kicked in big time once we were under that baking Italian sun. We had waited all year for this.

'Are you thinking of The Vanish?' Holly murmured under her breath to me as we lay by the pool.

'Nn-nn.' I shook my head. 'I think it just vanished.'

MARK

Because I don't see much of my dad – he is a very successful businessman and spends a lot of time doing deals – I normally like to talk to Godfather Gideon about the days when he and my father were young together.

This time was different. Wiki turned up at my house after breakfast, a neat little rucksack on his back. Gideon was there by mid-morning. He and my mother have never got along, so it was not exactly a warm, social occasion. He left his taxi running as we said goodbye to Mum and climbed in.

On our way towards Paddington Station, none of us was in the mood for conversation.

MRS SARA BLISS

Gideon Burrowes, Mark's godfather, is not what one would call normal but I discovered during my marriage to Mark's father that he is essentially harmless. Mark sees so little of his father that I have always felt it does him good to be in male company.

But I had a niggling sense that things were what I call 'out of kilter' that morning. The little black boy, William Church, was a surprise – I couldn't think what Mark and he had in common. Then Gideon appeared, wearing a pair of very small dark glasses of the type hippies used to wear. Nothing felt quite as it should be.

It occurred to me, as they drove off, that I should have a word with Mark's father but he was somewhere in Dubai and I didn't have a number for him.

Nothing Mark Bliss had said prepared me for Gideon Burrowes. He was in his forties, I learned later, but he had this thick mop of straight grey hair that reached down to his shoulders.

He wore a dark, baggy suit that was probably made about a hundred years ago. Weirdest of all, he had these circular, metal-rimmed granny glasses that you see in photographs of hippies back in the 1960s. It was difficult not to laugh but somehow one sensed that this was a man who was not too heavily into joking.

He hardly said a word after he had picked us both up at Mark's house.

EVA JOHANSSON

Trix was not herself. I can see that now. Too silent. Too pale. Too moody. At the time though, I was very preoccupied by what was happening in La-La-Land, better known as Hollywood! My agent had rung to tell me that I was up for a second screen test on a major movie. There were calls. There were plans. Frankly, I couldn't wait to get on the plane back to America.

I drove Trix to Paddington Station. I found her a seat opposite a nice old couple. She had been worried about missing the train and so, of course, we were ten minutes early. I said goodbye.

Trix's last words to me were, 'See you, Mummy. Look after yourself.'

This is very hard for me – there is no pain like a mother's pain.

MRS GARNETT

We like to be in good time for the journey home. When this tall, elegant woman, talking rather loudly in a foreign accent, swept into the carriage at Paddington, we rather hoped she would not be sitting opposite us.

MR GARNETT

But luckily it was only her daughter, a quiet girl in a Feed-the-World T-shirt, who sat down. She was firm about one thing – she didn't want to sit alone, she told her her mother. With a little smile in our direction, she chose the seat opposite ours. Only later we discovered that she was the famous little Trixie Bell.

MRS GARNETT

As the mother fussed about a bit, putting the girl's suitcase on the rack, asking her rather loudly whether she wanted the window seat and so on, I began to think I recognized her from somewhere. Had she been a newscaster years ago – or maybe one of those weathergirls? I remember thinking that there was something not entirely natural about her. She was like someone acting the part of a mother rather badly.

Then, with a couple of showy mwa-mwa kisses, she was off.

MR GARNETT

Trixie Bell waved out of the window as her mother walked off, but the mother never looked back. It was rather sad, I thought.

EVA JOHANSSON

I had a plane to catch. I was on a rather tight schedule. Jason rang from America as I got back to the car. The film I was auditioning for had been mentioned in the *Hollywood Reporter*. He particularly remembers that I was quite upset about saying goodbye to Trix.

MARK

Though I say it myself, we looked well scary. I was wearing a baseball cap and a puffa jacket that my father had given me for a sailing trip that had never happened. I had a white silk scarf wrapped around my neck that I was going to pull up over the lower part of my face like a bandit in a cowboy film. Then I had these big reflector shades that I wear for skiing.

Wiki looked even creepier than usual. He had on a black trilby hat, cheap dark glasses and a long black coat. He was like someone going to a funeral.

MRS GARNETT

After a couple of minutes, the girl casually started looking for something in her jeans pockets. Then she checked in the coat she had put on the seat beside her. She grew increasingly panicky.

MR GARNETT

'My mobile,' she said. 'I've left my mobile in the car.'

My wife tried to calm her. 'Don't worry, love. There's always a landline.'

MRS GARNETT

'I must have my mobile,' she said in quite a trembly little voice. She looked at her watch. 'Could you just keep an eye on my things?' she said to me.

My husband said, 'Well, the train goes in eight minutes.'

'I'll be right back,' she said. And she was gone, out of the carriage, running down the platform.

That was the last we ever saw of her.

EVA JOHANSSON

That blinking cellphone. She was always losing it. I found it on the back seat about an hour later when I had parked the car at Heathrow Airport. Of course, it was too late to do anything about it.

WIKI

It was a simple plan, but a good one.

There would be the lost phone. Trix would make sure that she was seen getting off the train. Once through the ticket barrier, she would run to Praed Street outside the station. Again, she would make sure people saw her.

We would be waiting in the taxi, looking out for her.

GODFATHER GIDEON

Why we were obliged to wait around the corner before picking up Mark's other friend slightly puzzled me. But, no questions. That's the thing.

WIKI

And suddenly there was Trix. She was pacing backwards and forwards outside the station like a real little girl lost. I'll give her that – she was a great actress.

I leaned forward from the back seat and pointed her out to Mr Burrowes. He drove the taxi forward. Trix saw us and started walking away from us but near the edge of the pavement.

As we pulled up beside her, Mark opened the back door of the taxi. She turned, surprised.

Together, Mark and I reached forward and grabbed her.

'What?' she shouted so loudly that Mark and I let go of her. 'No! No!' she screamed. She looked at us furiously. Then she sort of fell into the taxi as if we had grabbed her. We slammed the door.

Mr Burrowes looked around, a bit surprised.

'This is Trix,' said Mark, trying unsuccessfully to sound jolly. 'She's a bit of a joker.'

'How do you do, Trix?' said Mr Burrowes.

'Hi,' said Trix, sitting on the floor.

'There's plenty of room on the—'

'Let's go, Gideon,' said Mark more urgently now.

The taxi moved off, the slowest getaway car there has ever been.

I glanced back. A mother with a pram was staring after us.

TRACY BROWN

It seemed to happen in slow motion, like a terrible dream. I noticed this old taxi coming down the road. It was driven by this man with dark glasses and long grey hair – a real psycho type. I couldn't see them, but I sensed he had really cold eyes. I was just thinking to myself, That's no taxi driver, when he pulled up beside this young girl and the back door of the cab opened.

I remember the girl screaming 'No!', and then these two people in dark glasses – small gangster types, one black and one white – grabbed her. The taxi waited there for a few seconds – I can only think that the poor little girl was struggling. But before I could do anything, it was gone.

You know the creepiest thing? He drove away slowly, that man. As if he were enjoying every moment of it.

Poor Trixie. Poor little Trixie Bell. If only I could have

done something for her. I was so shocked I wasn't able to catch the registration number.

WIKI

According to one of my favourite websites, totallyweirdfacts. com, the average person going about his daily business gets caught on security cameras 672 times a day.

So we all kept our shades on until we were well out of London. Trix lay on the floor of the taxi. Godfather Gideon kept driving. He never said a word.

GODFATHER GIDEON

I suppose it was not entirely what one would expect at the start of a godchild's stay, but I've always believed that individuality is the lifeblood of a society and I liked the idea that Mark was involved in some escapade of his own. Any worthwhile life has its share of adventures.

As the taxi trundled on to the motorway, I heard the three of them laughing. I closed the little window behind me. I find the laughter of children slightly upsetting.

MARK

We had done it. We were on our way. When the Trixter clambered off the floor and sat down between Wiki and me, it was as if the craziness of what we were doing hit us for the first time.

'That was the most pathetic piece of kidnapping I've ever seen,' she muttered. 'Talk about a couple of powder puffs. I had to put up a struggle against myself.'

''Ere, you.' I pointed at her, like some tough guy on TV. 'Shut it!'

That was when the three of us lost it. We couldn't stop laughing for about five minutes.

Wiki was falling about so much that his dark glasses misted up. When he took them off, his cheeks were wet with tears.

At that moment he looked so different from the speccy nerd I thought I knew at Cathcart that I started wondering how he had got into this. Holly and the Beanpole were Trix's best friends, I was up for a little adventure with Godfather Gideon. The mystery was Wiki.

I asked him where he had told his parents he was going. That wiped the smile off his face.

'I told them I'm staying with you.'

'Me?' I laughed. 'But we're not even friends . . . I mean, we hardly know each other.'

'I know we're not friends,' he said. 'But you're the sort of person my mother always hoped I'd meet at Cathcart. Someone who's all the things I'm not.'

'Yeah?' I nodded. That made sense.

'If they want to contact me, they'll call my mobile. It might be an idea for you to talk to them.'

I shrugged. 'Fine,' I said. 'I'm good at snowing parents.'

WIKI

We had been travelling two hours and maybe it was the

75

excitement, but I was beginning to feel in need of the lavatory.

I pulled back the little window behind Godfather Gideon's head.

'Mr Burrowes,' I said, 'I was wondering if I could have a comfort break.'

For some reason, Trix and Mark started to laugh.

'A comfort break?' he said. 'Is that what they call it these days?'

'He means he wants to take a pee, Gideon,' said Mark.

'Thank you, Mark. I worked that out for myself. I'll stop at the next service station.'

Suddenly Trix was whispering in Mark's ear.

GODFATHER GIDEON

I suppose it should have occurred to me that something was going on when Mark suggested that, if we had to stop, it should be at a small village garage.

On the other hand, the reason that he gave made perfect sense. Those motorway service stations are riddled with cameras, he said. Every one of them was sending back images to the government.

When my godson was small, I had told him how the government is watching us every minute of the day. Until then, I had rather thought he had taken the information as some kind of joke. I was delighted that he was beginning to understand the kind of thing I had been talking about.

WIKI

Here's a tip for anyone planning to do a kidnapping: take sandwiches.

By the time we were off the motorway and heading into the mountains of Wales, we were starving. Godfather Gideon had bought himself some chocolate at the filling station but, to our surprise and disappointment, he ate every bit himself.

'Godfather Gideon believes in self-sufficiency,' Mark explained. These words were destined to haunt us in the future.

JADE

The holiday in Italy: it was not a blast.

The elements were there from the moment we arrived.

Sun, scenery, swimming pool? Check.

Ice-cold juice from freshly squeezed oranges? Yep.

Not too many adults around asking how school was and have we any ideas about careers? No problemo.

But as we lay there in the sun, sipping squash and soaking up the sun, all we could think of was what was going down back in England. It was V Day and we were catching some rays beside a swimming pool.

HOLLY

Secretly, both of us were hoping that something would go wrong. Maybe Wiki would mess up or Mark would blab to an adult.

But deep in our hearts we knew. We're talking about Trix Johansson-Bell here, the one and only TJB. When she puts her mind to something, it's going to happen.

WIKI

'It's relaxed and it's not relaxed,' Mark said about Hill Farm, where his godfather lived.

'The house is like this kind of brambled-up hideaway in the hillside,' he said, trying again. 'Being there is like becoming a wild animal.'

'A wild animal? What are you talking about, Mark?' said Trix.

'I can't explain,' said Mark. 'I'm not very good at explanations.'

Trix sighed and looked out of the window. 'Tell me something I don't know,' she muttered.

We climbed higher. At first, when the taxi came to a halt on a steep incline, I thought that it had broken down. Then we turned sharp left up a bumpy little track with trees crowding in on both sides.

After 200 metres the taxi trundled into a sort of grove.

'That's it,' said Mark, pointing to a larger-than-usual bramble patch. Looking more closely, I saw that beneath the undergrowth was a house. As we drew closer, I noticed that the front door was open. From the darkness inside, a cat appeared as if it owned the place, then wandered off into the grass.

Gideon switched off the engine, stepped out of the cab and, without even glancing in our direction, walked into the house.

We got out and looked around. There was no other place in sight but, to one side of Hill Farm, there was a barn and some sheds. We walked through the open door into a large, dusty kitchen.

Gideon had taken a mug from a large stack of unwashed dishes in the sink, and busied himself with the kettle, making a cup of tea.

We stood uneasily in the centre of the room, looking around us. The pots and pans in the kitchen, the ancient old cooker, were like something out of a history project.

'I'll show you around,' Mark said. 'Is that all right, Gideon?'

'Hm?' He poured some boiling water into his cup. 'Oh, right. Make yourselves at home. I've got to catch up on some work.'

And he was out of the door and gone.

'Your godfather seems in a bit of a bad mood,' said Trix.

'He lives in a world of his own,' said Mark. 'Which is a good thing, right?'

'I suppose so,' said Trix. She looked at her watch. 'I wonder if the news has broken.'

'We could check on TV,' I said.

Mark winced. 'What TV is that?' he said.

MARK

I began to worry about the TV thing. Gideon's weird ideas about the government watching us had helped us so far, but his belief that televisions were cameras in disguise looked as if it was going to be a problem.

Eventually, rooting about in the attic of the house, I found a small black and white set with its own little aerial. When I asked Gideon about it, he told me he had bought it when he was a student. At first he refused to let us try it out but, when I promised that we would leave it in the attic, where nothing could be revealed to government spies, he agreed.

It worked – just. When, the day after we arrived, the three of us gathered in the darkness to look at the small, fuzzy black and white images on the tiny screen, it was as if we had gone back in time and were like a gang of children in some ancient storybook.

We watched the news again and again. There was nothing about Trix.

WIKI

Five weird things about the countryside:

1. The noise. No one warns you about this. Birds start singing their beaks off while it's still dark in the morning. I'm a light sleeper, and after a couple of days I was missing life at home in the city. At least you can get a decent night's sleep there.

2. It's impossible to relax. Gideon was up as soon as it was light and spent most of the day in his work-shed. When he came out, there was always something he had to do – collect eggs from the hens, dig up vegetables, fetch logs, fix up a piece of machinery. Soon he got us at it too. Mark had to cut some long grass with his scythe. I was weeding the vegetable patch. Trix was filling in potholes in the drive. This was not how I imagined our great adventure panning out.

3. It's smelly. In the house it was the cats. Outside it was the cattle. In the country different types of lavatory smells are wafting around all the time.

4. You talk quite a lot. Because there were no computers, and at first no TV, the three of us ended up talking to one another. It took a bit of getting used to.

5. It's very, very violent. Hardly an hour goes by in the country without some creature dying a horrible death. It might be a mouse, caught by one of the cats, or a rat in one of Gideon's traps. On the second day we were there, he discovered that we didn't have any dinner. He wandered out of the kitchen, there was a squawk from nearby and he came back with this chicken hanging from his hand, *still twitching*.

'I'm going to be sick,' said Trix.

Gideon allowed a rare smile to cross his face. 'Who wants to learn how to pluck and gut a hen?' he asked.

Trix pursed her lips and gave Gideon the evil eye. 'Pluck? Gut? That's disgusting.'

'No supper for you then?' Gideon asked.

Trix frowned. That was another thing about the country. It made you hungry all the time.

'It's just so *uncivilized*,' Trix muttered.

Mark caught my eye and we began laughing. I had to admit that away from Cathcart College, Mark Bliss was almost all right.

GODFATHER GIDEON

I have never been able to grasp the concept of holidays. Sit around, stare into space, yawn, scratch your bum – *but why*? Surely everybody knows that doing nothing is far more tiring than working. There was no possible way that I could look after the children – I was already late with an order from Canada for a bowed rocker made from black walnut.

So I encouraged Mark and his two friends to explore the place.

And here was a bit of a surprise: it was the black kid with specs, the one they called 'Wiki', who was quickest to understand the point of living in the countryside. He spent most of the day outside. Then, that evening, I noticed he was looking through my books about birds and trees.

HOLLY

I'll be honest. I was not totally thrilled that Trix had destroyed my holiday. I love Tuscany. The villa is unbelievable. I see the weeks there as my reward for putting up with Cathcart all year. Even my parents manage to chill after a few days, although my father spends an hour worshipping the great god of BlackBerry every morning.

At first we would sneak off to the media room now and then to check on the news channels whether there had been anything about a kidnapping in London. By the second day, we were beginning to assume that, perhaps thanks to a late burst of sanity, the plan had been abandoned.

Late that afternoon I said to Jade as she lay in the sun, 'Maybe we should check the news on TV.'

'Mm?'

'There could be something about Trix.'

'Mm.'

'On the other hand, we could just turn over, toast our other side and forget about it for a while.'

'*Mm.*'

What could I say?

JADE

Here's the thing. Africa's a long way from Italy.

At that moment Holly and I were having pretty much the same thought.

Maybe nothing had happened back in England. Maybe we'd forget the deal we cut with Trix to come home two days after the news broke about the kidnap. Maybe we wouldn't go home after all. Maybe we'd pretend not to have seen the news. Maybe something really important would turn up which meant we had to stay on holiday.

Tell you what. We'd sleep on it and see how we felt in the morning.

EVA JOHANSSON

I'll never forget that day. It was late morning when the big news came through.

I was in line for a part in a major production starring Jennifer Lopez! With a megastar on board, Hollywood studios were taking the project seriously. I had been through a bad run recently – even my agent wasn't returning my calls – but that morning I sensed that my luck was about to change. I had once met Jenny (as she likes to be called). Maybe she could have a word about me to the casting director.

But then, an hour or so later, another call came through and suddenly the idea of appearing in a major international production began to seem almost insignificant.

My daughter was missing. No one had seen her for two days. It was a mother's worst nightmare.

As the police said later, luck was against us. When Trix had first disappeared, I was in the air, flying to Los Angeles. Then the summer camp she was meant to be attending only left a message on my landline number – as if busy people can wait by the phone all day! No one thought to call the Drunk, Trix's father (or maybe I forgot to leave his number with the camp – I can't think of everything).

Then I had been tied up with the possibility of appearing with Jenny on screen and had not been taking calls. It was bad, bad timing.

PETE BELL

It was late afternoon when the bell rang. It had been a rough week and, after a long night, the phone had been off the hook. When I opened the door, a dark-haired man and a woman were standing there. One glance, and I could tell they were coppers. In my business, you develop a sixth sense for these things.

They said that Eva had given them my address; that they needed to talk to me about my daughter. I invited them into my flat. I could tell they weren't exactly impressed by the state of it.

DETECTIVE INSPECTOR BARRY CARTWRIGHT

Mr Peter Bell, the girl's father, lived in what I would call a 'disordered' state. Dishes in the sink, full ashtrays, empty bottles. His breath stank of whisky although it was teatime when I paid him a visit.

After five minutes it was clear that he would be unable to help us. He hadn't seen his daughter for over a month and didn't even realize she was meant to be at a summer camp.

Normally, a father in this kind of condition, with a chaotic lifestyle, might have been a suspect, but it was difficult to take that idea seriously. How could a man who forgot to shave, couldn't remember the date of his only child's birthday and had his fly buttons undone throughout the entire police interview be organized enough to arrange a kidnapping?

The only mystery in my mind is how on earth this sad

character could have been married to a beautiful and successful woman like Eva Johansson.

PETE BELL

I need a drink. That was my first thought after the cops had left. I always need a drink, it's true, but now I *really* needed a drink.

How could this happen? How could someone as strong and independent as Trix be snatched from the street and disappear? It didn't make sense. Of all the people I know, she is the least likely to be a victim.

I rang Trix's mother. She was too upset to speak to me. (I noticed later that she wasn't too upset to talk to the press.)

The phone began ringing the next day. Journalists. I answered their questions as best I could. By then, thanks to the whisky, I wasn't thinking too straight.

WIKI

Two days, three days. Nothing.

Later we discovered that it had taken time for word of Trix's kidnapping to reach her mother and that the police had kept it quiet for another twenty-four hours.

We, of course, were panicking.

'I may not mean much, but you'd think someone would notice that I had gone missing,' Trix said as we walked around Godfather Gideon's three small fields for about the hundredth time. She was only half joking.

Then, on the evening of the third day, while Gideon was

working in his shed, we climbed the ladder to the attic and gathered around the TV for the early evening news.

First item. We were looking at a photograph of Trix.

'There is growing concern following the disappearance of a schoolgirl three days ago,' the newsreader said in the worried voice that means really bad news is on its way. 'Fourteen-year-old Trixie Bell was last seen outside Paddington Station, from where she was due to catch a train to a summer camp. Witnesses say that she was snatched by men using a London taxi. Trixie is the daughter of the actress Eva Johansson, who is married to the prominent sports agent Jason Everleigh.'

'Trixie!' Trix muttered. 'I haven't been called that since I was seven.'

There was some film of the street where the kidnap had taken place. Then a policeman was interviewed in front of a crowd of reporters.

'It does appear that this young girl was taken against her will,' he said. 'Trixie's parents are currently in Los Angeles and are returning to England at this moment in time. We would ask anyone with information as to the whereabouts of Trixie Bell to contact our incident room as a matter of urgency.'

A number appeared on the screen.

'Why has news of this only emerged today?' one of the journalists called out.

The policeman hesitated. 'We are giving no further details of this case until we have interviewed the parents of the missing girl.' Several of the reporters tried to ask other questions.

'However,' the policeman continued, 'it does seem that there was a problem of communication, which has delayed our investigations.' He looked into the camera. 'I would repeat that anyone who can help us with our enquiries should contact us – in confidence, if necessary.'

The news report switched to America, where Trix's mum and stepfather were filmed at an airport. Escorted by three serious-looking men in suits, they were making their way towards the check-in desk. Both looked pale and wore dark glasses.

'Eva, have you any message for your daughter?' someone called out.

Trix's mother slowed, then turned. 'I just want her home,' she said. 'She's the best daughter in the world. She never gets into trouble. I don't understand any of this.'

Someone tried to ask another question, but the men in tight suits escorted her away.

'Poor Mum,' Trix said.

There was a brief conversation between the newsreader and the reporter who was standing where the policeman had been interviewed.

Trixie was just a normal young girl, the reporter said. Because her parents were wealthy, there was a theory that she was being held to ransom. 'Obviously, the more time goes by without any contact from possible kidnappers, the more concerned the police are becoming for her safety.'

'Here's that number again,' said the newsreader. 'Witnesses who can provide any information regarding the whereabouts of Trixie Bell are asked to contact the police.'

EVA JOHANSSON

We were grateful that the detective in charge of the case was Detective Inspector Barry Cartwright, who has handled high-profile cases before. He understands how important the media can be in cases like this. It was Barry who said that we should call her 'Trixie' rather than 'Trix' when talking to the press. Getting the public on your side, making them care, was very important, he said.

'Trix' sounded a bit tough, maybe even a bit boyish. 'Trixie' was more vulnerable. I trusted him. The police know about these things.

WIKI

We switched the TV off when the news moved on to the next item, a big train crash in Spain. For a few moments we sat in silence, each of us with the same thought in our mind.

What have we done?

It was Mark who recovered first.

'All right there, *Trixie*?' he said

'Trixie – what *is* that? I hate that name,' said Trix. 'And they chose the worst photograph of me. It made me look like a spoilt little rich girl.'

'Your mum was a bit upset,' I said quietly. It was meant to be a helpful remark but, as soon as the words left my mouth, Trix's eyes were filled with tears. She wiped them away angrily.

'Well done, Wik,' said Mark.

'I was only saying. I just thought that—'

'This is about Africa.' Trix spoke quietly. 'Let's just remember all the mothers in Ethiopia and Mali, and how they feel when their children actually die.'

'Except –' I tried to put it as sensitively as I could – 'she is your mum.'

'Maybe we could get word to her that you're not dead,' said Mark.

Trix laughed angrily. 'What, give her a call on the mobile and say everything is fine? We're just hanging out in Wales with a madman plucking chickens?'

'Email?' I suggested. 'Find an Internet cafe somewhere?'

'No.' It was Trix who was first to pull herself together and think straight.

'I once saw a film where the gang sent a message with bits of newspaper,' she said. 'They cut up words from different newspapers to make a message. That way there was no handwriting or anything.'

'They'd be able to tell where it came from,' I said. 'From the postmark.'

We sat there in the gloom, each of us trying to think of an answer to this impossible question: how do you kidnap someone without upsetting her mum?

Downstairs we could hear Gideon making clattering sounds in the kitchen, which meant he was making supper.

Without a word, we stood up. It should have been a good moment – the kidnap was on the news, we were in business – but suddenly there was this giant weight on our shoulders.

There was no going back now.

MARK

If *The Godfather Gideon Cookbook* existed, its basic ingredients would be this:

1. Kill something.

2. Do disgusting things to remove its fur/feathers/innards.

3. Throw it in a big saucepan.

4. Look in the fridge for any vegetables you've collected from the kitchen garden.

5. Chop them up into the saucepan.

6. Boil it until it smells really good.

Meals produced by Gideon all look the same – i.e. revolting – but they taste good in different ways. After the first day, we just closed our eyes and got on with it. I've never eaten anything better.

But the evening when Trix made the TV news we were right off our food. Gideon is not usually the greatest at mealtime chatter – normally he'd just sit at the end of the table, shovelling in food and thinking about rocking chairs, but that night he surprised us.

GODFATHER GIDEON

Something was up. I smelt it as surely as a hare smells a fox.

I knew Mark liked his adventures. The first time he came here, he climbed the big walnut tree next to the house and nearly brained himself when he fell off a branch. Children need freedom, country air in their lungs, mud on their hands. A bit of wildness in their early years will harden them for the evil world they are growing up in.

But at dinner that night, I began to worry. They were too quiet, too pale, too generally guilty in the way they looked and moved about. There was something odd too about all those trips to the attic.

I was almost tempted to break my golden rule and ask them questions.

Instead, I gave them some work to do.

WIKI

There was this low rumble from the end of the table. Godfather Gideon was preparing to do something unusual. He was going to talk to us.

'Time for you sprogs to earn your keep,' he said, his eyes darting around at us under his grey thatch of hair.

'Gideon, it's holiday-time,' said Mark, rather too cheerfully. 'Can't we just chillax for a few days?'

'Chillax.' Gideon seemed to be chewing this over in his mind like a bit of rabbit from the stew we were eating.

'It means chill and relax,' said Trix. 'Like, take it easy.'

He breathed in sharply through his nose, another of his little habits. 'If you want to . . . chillax, I'll drive you to the station tomorrow and you can take the train home. At Hill Farm, we work. Don't we, Mark?'

'If you say so, Gideon.' Mark's answer was just this side of rudeness, but only just.

'So. The tasks. Shopping. The village is two miles away. I have two old bicycles in the shed, which I shall make good before breakfast tomorrow. I shall give you directions and expect full supplies for the house. You pay, of course.'

'Of course,' said Mark.

Daringly, I mentioned that there was a bit of a steep hill to the farm. Wouldn't coming back carrying provisions –?

Gideon gave me a cold look with his piecing blue eyes. The words froze in my throat.

'Then there's firewood. You collect. You saw. You stack.'

'That's one for you, Wik,' said Mark. 'You need building up.'

'Cooking.' He looked at Trix.

'Just because I'm a girl,' she said, 'it doesn't mean that—'

'I don't care who does what. If you prefer, you can be in charge of hunting.'

'Hunting? That is so . . .' Almost for the first time since I had known her, Trix seemed lost for words. '. . . so twentieth century.'

Gideon stabbed a piece of meat on his plate. 'You eat, you hunt,' he said. 'I've got a four-ten shotgun one of you can take.'

We looked at one another.

'It's fun,' he said. 'Where have you children been all your lives? Rabbit, pigeon, pheasant, woodcock. If it moves and it looks tasty, you can shoot it.'

'I've never used a gun before,' I said in a quiet voice.

'Wimp,' said Mark. 'I'm a good shot, I'll be the hunter.'

'Then we'll need someone to pluck, skin and gut. There are the snares to check for rabbits.'

'Snares? That is so cruel, Gideon,' said Trix with a bit of her old spirit.

'Your choice,' he said. 'Finally, rats.'

'Please tell me you're not saying we eat rats here,' said Trix.

Gideon raised an eyebrow. 'It's a thought. I believe stewed rat is rather a delicacy around the world. But we'll only have to eat them if the hunter fails to hunt. No, all one of you needs to do is shoot them in the evenings and early mornings around the chicken shed. They're taking too many eggs and chicks.'

'Couldn't you just poison them?' asked Trix.

He looked at her. 'Now *that's* twentieth century,' he said. 'Poison is a slow, painful death. When owls pick them up, they get poisoned too. It's a positively barbarian way to keep numbers down.'

'We'll probably have shot all the owls anyway,' Trix muttered.

Gideon glowered for a moment. 'I shall devote tomorrow to training,' he said. 'After that, it's up to you. That's the way it is at Hill Farm. No free rides.' He returned to his meal. It was a big speech by his standards. 'Let me know who's doing what tomorrow at breakfast,' he muttered as he chewed.

MARK

So that night, the first night after the news of the Trixter's disappearance hit the media big time, we ended up in the bedroom which I shared with Wiki, not discussing the kidnap at all but deciding who was going to shop or shoot or cook or snare or kill rats.

It began to occur to me that staying with Gideon had not been such a great idea after all.

WIKI

The scary thing about Godfather Gideon was that he never ever joked. For him, we weren't children at all. We were mini-adults. If we had said that maybe allowing children to wander around with guns was not the safest idea, or asking them to put their hands into the bodies of dead animals to take out innards was a bit on the disgusting side, he would simply have looked at us as if we were mad.

He was a sort of caveman. He lived in a different world from the rest of us. Like it or not, we were in that world for the next few days. There was no escape.

Some decisions were easy. Because Trix's face was all over the papers, there was no question of her being seen in the village.

Mark fancied himself as a killer. Grumpily, with many mutterings about sexist men, Trix agreed to do the cooking.

Which, uh-oh, left me with the preparation – the skinning and gutting.

We couldn't get our heads around the whole rat thing.

HOLLY

It was lucky that my parents and their friends were nowhere near the villa's television room when Trix's face first loomed up on the big screen. They might have been ever so slightly surprised to hear Jade reacting to news that one of her friends had been kidnapped as if she were watching a football game and her team had just scored a goal.

'Whoa, result. Yessss.' She punched the air. 'They did it.'

We had been worried that the news had not broken sooner. Now that it had, there was almost nothing else. We got several out-of-date pictures of Trix, who now seemed to be called 'Trixie'. There was an interview with Miss Fothergill, who said what a marvellous person she was. Trix's mother and stepfather were filmed outside their house after flying back from America. At one point, the good-looking detective in charge of the case gazed into the camera and asked anyone with information about Trixie to get in touch with the police.

'I don't think so, buddy,' said Jade.

I pressed the remote and the screen turned black. Although the sun was still outside, the blinds were down and the air conditioning made the room cool.

'I can't believe that they actually did it,' I said.

Jade did an imitation of Wiki blinking behind his glasses. 'Hello, my name is William Church and I'm a kidnapper,' she said in a geeky voice.

We fell about.

'But you know what this means,' I said, sitting up and trying to think straight about the new situation. 'Our holiday is over.'

'Two days,' said Jade. 'We agreed to give it two days after the news broke.'

'At that point we'll be too upset by the news to enjoy ourselves in Italy and will just have to go home.'

That cracked us up too.

WIKI

The next day, Mark and I rode two heavy black bikes with big wicker baskets on the handlebars down to the village shop – or 'Mrs Phillips's', as Godfather Gideon preferred to call it.

In fact, we almost missed it. The village turned out to be a few little houses with neat gardens in the front of them at the bottom of the hill. As we raced past them, I noticed that one of the buildings had a Post Office sign outside it.

'Mrs Phillips!' Mark screamed, and we screeched to a halt, laughing. It was definitely a shop, we now saw, although the only thing in the window was a cat, fast asleep.

There were other things, odd things, about Mrs Phillips's:

1. You didn't have to lock your bikes up when you went inside. It took Mark and me several days to believe this.

2. The door opened with a little ting-a-ling noise from a bell attached to it.

3. It was so dark in there that you could hardly see what you were buying. (This was quite often a good thing.)

4. Sometimes you picked up an item and it looked as if it

98

has been there since the end of World War Two.

5. No one just walked into the village shop, bought something and left. They would potter about the dusty shelves. When they eventually reached Mrs Phillips behind the till they would discuss the weather for about half an hour, then tell each other some really interesting piece of gossip ('Did you hear that Mrs White's cat has passed away?' 'What, Mrs White that was Miss Pink?' 'That's the one. It was only twelve and all.' 'What do they think it was then?' 'Oh, Mr Brown says it's the weather.' 'Terrible weather we've been having lately,' etc., etc., etc.). Then they would realize they had forgotten something, so Mrs Phillips had to go and look for it 'out the back'. Then they needed a lottery ticket. Then they counted out the money in change very, very slowly. Mark said it was no wonder everyone in the country looks so old. Most of them have turned grey waiting to be served in their village shop.

6. Mrs Phillips is about 150 years old and has a beard.

But none of this was what we noticed that day. On the front page of all the newspapers, laid out on a low shelf at the front of the shop, was the same photograph of Trix.

As casually as we could, we crouched down to look more closely. One headline read 'TAXI KIDNAP OF ACTRESS'S DAUGHTER', another 'FIND LITTLE TRIXIE'. One even had 'OUR LITTLE ANGEL'.

'Little angel?' Mark murmured under his breath. 'I've heard it all now.'

We bought three newspapers – one serious, two trashy –

then bought the rest of the shopping.

At some point a woman in her sixties (a youngster in this village) walked in and began to chat with Mrs Phillips at the till.

As we approached, she smiled and said, 'You go ahead, you boys. We're just passing the time of day.'

Moving with the speed of an alpine glacier, Mrs Phillips took out each item, examined it, then tapped the price into the till. When she reached the newspapers at the bottom of the basket, she gazed sadly down at Trix for a moment.

'Terrible business, that young girl,' she said.

Before we could think of the right answer, the other woman standing nearby made a tutting noise.

'Taxi-driver, they say,' she said. 'You get some rough types driving them taxis.'

'You know what I'd do to people like that?' The shopkeeper's beard seemed to be trembling with anger. 'I'd lock them in a house and then I'd torch it. Burn them to a crisp, I would. That would teach them.'

'It would,' said the other woman. 'You know what? Hanging's too good for them.'

'Unless you hanged them really, really slowly,' said Mrs Phillips.

'Now that's a job I'd like to do.'

'Me too.'

I cleared my throat. Annoyed at having her torture daydreams interrupted, Mrs Phillips tapped in the price of the newspapers. 'You don't want to be reading any of that stuff. Not on your holidays.' She smiled, revealing her three remaining teeth. 'Where are you staying then?'

'With Gideon Burrowes,' said Mark.

'Ah, Gideon, there's a character.' Mrs Phillips smiled,

revealing her front teeth. 'A man of few words, as we say in these parts.'

'Yeah.' We took the bags of shopping and made for the door.

'Gideon won't be reading those papers,' the woman shopper said, a look of glittering suspicion in her eye. 'Gideon hasn't read a paper for years. He doesn't believe in them, does he, Mrs Phillips?'

'No,' said Mrs Phillips. 'No, he doesn't, come to think of it.'

The four of us stood for a moment like actors on a stage when one of them has forgotten their lines.

'Football!' I blurted out. 'The papers are for us. We're really big fans of football, aren't we, Mark?'

'Ye-es,' said Mark.

'And we like to read about our team. In all the papers.'

Before the two women could say anything else, we blundered out of the door, scrambled on to our bikes and began the cruel uphill journey back to Hill Farm.

MARK

At first, when we brought the newspapers home and took them up to the attic, Trix seemed cheerful – excited even. She complained about the photograph that had been used, laughed at all the mistakes in the stories about her.

But later that afternoon I found her sitting alone under an apple tree in the orchard, staring over the valley. I said something about how the great Trixter plot was going to plan.

'I guess so,' she said quietly. "But I can't believe those headlines. What was all that about Trixie? And since when did I become a little angel?'

'That's newspapers for you. They've got to come up with some kind of headline. What would you have put in their place?'

Trix thought for a moment, then smiled. 'I'd have put "MISSING, BELIEVED CRAZY". At least there's a bit of truth in that.'

I laughed. 'So now what?' I asked.

'We get Holly and Jade here.'

Oh, *great*, I thought. 'Great,' I said.

'Then we'll just have to see what happens.' She turned to me suddenly. 'We are doing the right thing, aren't we, Mark?'

I laughed. 'It's kind of late to be having second thoughts,' I said.

She sighed and went back to staring into space.

'It was a good plan,' I said. 'Remember the starving kids.'

She nodded. 'That's what matters, not me. The children of Mwanduna.'

'Right.'

We sat in silence for a moment.

What, I wondered, was going on out there beyond the mountains?

V Day + 5

EVA JOHANSSON

In my line of work, the ringing of the phone is like a heartbeat. It stops, and you know you're dead.

By now, Jason and I were back in England. The phone rang and rang yet I felt I was drowning – drowning in my own tears. It seemed that everybody wanted to talk about this terrible Trixie business.

Some calls were from famous friends offering to help (I could mention names but I won't). Others were from ordinary friends. Detective Inspector Cartwright rang me to 'keep me in the loop' as he put it, about the progress of police investigations (I would say no progress at all). Then there were the newspapers, on and on about Little Trixie this, Little Trixie that. 'What about a mother's pain?' I wanted to ask them. 'Why don't you write about that?'

Then, after two days back in England, something rather interesting happened. My American agent Lori rang me to tell me that she had received calls from people in the business asking her whether I was still working. I was too upset about Trixie to listen carefully, but I do recall Lori mentioned a major player in Hollywood who, for reasons of confidentiality, I shall call Leonardo DiC. These people were not ringing out of sympathy for me, my agent said – merely that the news had reminded them of my talent.

Talent? Me? It was hardly the time to talk about my talent as a leading actress.

'Lori,' I said, 'listen to me. I am a mother. I am holding on to my life like a shipwrecked person clinging on to a raft in stormy seas. I know you're doing your job but right now I can only think of Trixie.'

'So I turn them down?'

'On the other hand,' I said, 'I know that I owe it to Jason, to you, to my public, to keep working when this nightmare is finished. What is it they say? The show must go on.'

Lori waited a moment, then said, 'So that's a yes, right? I keep listening to the offers?'

'Do what you must,' I said, emotion overcoming me once more. 'Do what you must.'

LORI MAPLETHORPE-MOORE

I'm not saying Eva was washed up as an actress at that point. People still remembered her from the 1980s. But, until the kidnap came along, I was being asked if she was available for anti-ageing-cream ads. You hear what I'm saying? The stuff about her daughter going missing gave her visibility. That's just the way show business works.

JASON EVERLEIGH

It was 'Welcome to the madhouse'. The phone rang. Eva got hysterical. And in the middle of all this, I'm on the phone to the States trying to do deals for my clients. I tell you, it was Nightmare City.

Then, just when I thought things couldn't get any worse,

guess who walked – maybe that should be 'staggered' – back into the picture.

The father. The big-time loser. The Drunk.

TRACY BROWN

I went to the police station to help them produce a computer simulation of the man who snatched poor little Trixie.

It was so frighteningly realistic that, when I saw it, I actually broke down in tears. Those horrible, horrible moments came flooding back.

When the newspapers showed the picture, the man I had seen was described as 'the Demon Taxi-Driver'. Yes, I thought, that's right, that's how he looked – like someone who had come from hell.

HOLLY

The strange, scary stuff that was appearing on the TV began to get to us. We had to keep reminding ourselves that Trix was tough. She was in control. She had never been Little Trixie. There was no such thing as a Demon Taxi-Driver.

The kidnap story was spiralling out of control.

JADE

Every day, the Little Trixie of the headlines seemed less like the Trix we knew. Every day, the theories about her disappearance grew wilder.

One day, Mr Hunky Policeman (who had started wearing a rather cool pair of dark glasses) mentioned that he had been told Trixie spent a lot of time online. His team had been 'working on the theory' that she had met some older bloke in a chat room and had been persuaded to see him.

'Yeah,' said Holly, her eyes on the screen. 'And we're now working on the theory that you're a total prat.'

Trix in a chat room, allowing herself to be stalked by some old geezer. How pathetic was that?

DETECTIVE INSPECTOR BARRY CARTWRIGHT

I regret I am not at liberty to divulge my source of information as regards the theory that someone was 'grooming' Trixie online. Suffice to say, my officers took it seriously enough at the time for me to mention it during my interviews. It was an important part of the developing picture.

PETE BELL

In the press reports, they referred to me as a 'former journalist'. That hurt. 'Former'? What was former about me? Every morning, when I awoke, I was still, in my poor, tired, aching brain, a journalist. I'd take a cup of black coffee and light the first cigarette of the day. I'd make my way to my desk, switch on the computer, switch on my brain, and wait.

And wait.

And wait.

A story. I just needed a story. Fifteen years ago, just before Trix was born, there were stories all around me. I travelled the world, writing about politics, war, people. I wasn't just hot. I was on fire. A Pete Bell story was guaranteed the front page of any newspaper. People envied me – my job, my beautiful wife, my daughter, my shining, golden future.

Now everything was grey and no story seemed to matter any more except the one I didn't want to tell – how a promising young journalist with a lovely and successful wife threw it all away.

It's always the same. After about an hour in front of the computer screen, it occurs to me, as if for the first time, that the engine might need a little lubrication. Yes. Just a small one. It will be a spark. Get the motor turning.

To the kitchen. Open the cupboard. Take out the whisky bottle. Pour a small glass. Knock it back in one gulp.

Ah. It burns. It makes me feel alive. I'm rolling now. In fact, I feel so much better that I'll take a second glass up with me to work.

So the day's slide into the haze begins.

Soon after Trix's disappearance appeared on the news, a journalist I used to work with rang me. He is now a big wheel on one of the national newspapers. He asked the usual questions about Trix and was just about to sign off when he said, after this telling little pause, 'What happened, Pete?'

I asked him what he meant.

'When we were on the newsdesk together, you cared about things – you cared too much sometimes. Now someone kidnaps your only child and you're sitting there, feeling sorry for yourself and getting drunk.'

'Instead of what exactly?'

'Instead of doing something. Instead of fighting. Instead of showing that caring about something – loving someone – doesn't mean a thing unless you take action. That was what the young Pete Bell would have done.'

I really didn't need that – a sermon. Not in my state. I swore at him and hung up. Poured myself another drink. It tasted sour in my mouth.

That night, I couldn't sleep. The conversation with my former friend kept coming back to me. Fighting. Taking action. Showing you care. That was what the young Pete Bell would have done.

The next morning I put in a call to Detective Inspector Cartwright, then left a message on my ex-wife's voicemail. I started making notes. Maybe I needed a little pick-me-up to help me think straight.

I made my way as usual towards the drinks cupboard, then gave it a swerve. I put the kettle on for a cup of coffee.

MISS FOTHERGILL

Those policemen! After I told them that Trix had spent a lot of time with her laptop that summer term, they just would not let it go. Who was she talking to? Did she have special online 'buddies'?

I told them again and again. She was concerned about world poverty. She was finding out how she could help. 'Buddies' were frankly the last thing on poor little Trix's mind. I'm not sure they believed me.

DETECTIVE INSPECTOR BARRY CARTWRIGHT

When you're in the business of fighting crime, you've seen it all. Civilians – teachers, parents – have no idea what their little darlings get up to. A fourteen-year-old girl worrying about Africa. No, no, no. That wasn't going to fly. It didn't compute.

PETE BELL

In the old days, when I was still someone, I would now and then get lost in a story, confused by all the information I had uncovered. There were so many theories as to why something happened, so many voices saying different things.

So I would get out a piece of paper and write down what I actually knew. Sometimes when the fog of opinion and speculation was lifted, I could see more clearly what had happened.

It was what I did next. I put aside everything I had read in the press or heard from the police about Trix, and thought of what I knew about her.

I had sensed from her occasional calls to me from school that there was something wrong, something missing in her life. Her mother ignored her. I was too awash with booze and self-pity to be of use. Her stepfather actively disliked her. There had been problems at school. Now she had disappeared.

What if this was not a kidnapping at all but a break for freedom? Maybe Trix had run away to start a new life. It would have been a wild thing to do, but Trix has never lacked courage.

I shared my thoughts with Barry Cartwright. It's fair to say that he was unimpressed.

DETECTIVE INSPECTOR BARRY CARTWRIGHT

Very often in these cases, the father is involved. Divorced. Bitter. On the skids. Drink problem. All these factors made Peter Bell what we police officers call 'unreliable'. When he popped in at a key part of our investigations and told us that he was convinced that little Trixie had run away of her own accord, we began to have our suspicions. We kept him under surveillance. Eva Johansson was convinced that we were wrong, but in this game you can't be too certain.

We had the Demon Taxi-Driver. Now we had the Dodgy Dad. I felt we were making progress.

MRS MAGGIE DE VRIESS

My daughter Holly has always been a caring person. Not surprisingly, the disappearance of her little friend began to take the gloss off her Italian holiday. She began to mooch about, watching TV rather than sitting by the pool. Both she and her American friend Jade seemed jumpy and ill at ease. I suspected that neither of them were sleeping as well as they should.

So when, one evening while we were having a barbecue on the terrazzo, Holly announced that she and Jade wanted to go home, we were not entirely surprised.

'But, darling,' I said, 'there's no one to go home to.

We're out here and Jade's parents will probably be at work all day.'

'We can stay with Mark Bliss,' she said coolly.

'Who exactly is Mark Bliss?' asked Geoff, my husband.

'He's a good friend of Trix's,' said Holly. 'And her other best friend William Church is staying with him at his godfather's place.'

I was not keen. It was not exactly a good time for young girls to be travelling about on their own.

'My mum will meet us at the airport,' Jade piped up. 'She'll put us on the train. It'll be cool.'

Later that night, Geoff and I discussed the matter. There was no way that we were going to interrupt our hard-earned holiday. I assumed Jade's mother was reliable. We agreed that we should call the godfather of this Mark Bliss and take it from there.

HOLLY

Had Jade just referred to her mum? I happened to know that her mother was on holiday on the other side of the world with her latest boyfriend.

I'll give that girl one thing. She had nerve.

GODFATHER GIDEON

Jeepers. More kids. This woman with a voice like a chainsaw rang from Italy. Mark had mentioned that the call was coming, so I was prepared. What a summer this was turning out to be.

'Oh well,' I said. 'I've got three of the little blighters here already. I suppose another two won't make a difference.'

To tell the truth, the idea was less painful than I might once have thought. Having Mark and his friends at Hill Farm had been almost enjoyable. Strange, that.

MRS DE VRIESS

Three? Who was the third? For a moment I was thrown. But Gideon Burrowes, the godfather, sounded a well-spoken man and I had his telephone number.

The third child, I assumed, was his own. Everyone has children, don't they?

WIKI

If it were not for the small fact that we were at the centre of a major international crime, those days at Hill Farm would have been pretty good. There were things to do all day – not just killing animals for supper, collecting eggs and firewood, but also swimming in a pond that was at the end of the fields, climbing trees. One day, after lunch, Gideon showed us how to whittle a piece of wood – ash is best – to make a catapult.

The sun shone. The cats basked themselves on the front doorstep. Birds (I found out from one of Gideon's books that they were swallows) swooped down over the courtyard and into the shed where he kept his tractor. Then there would be this mad twittering as they fed the chicks that were in a nest on a ledge. And off the adult swallows would go again.

Sometimes I just lay on the grass, feeling the sun on my skin and watching the swallows come and go. I felt alive.

MARK

I had been to Gideon's before and I knew the way it worked around there – look at the animals, drive the tractor, get used to the smell of cow-dung. It was fine in its way although, given the choice, I prefer real life.

The other two were less cool about it. Wiki morphed into this young gamekeeper-type, forever asking Gideon about some bird or flower that he found. 'Wow,' he'd say. 'Look at that – a lesser-spotted, crimson-breasted whatsit bird. They're really unusual.' At first I thought he was trying it on, but I began to realize that he was learning all sorts of stuff about the country every day. I had to admit it. Wiki was on his way to being a true straw-chewing country boy.

Ever since we had heard from Italy that Holly and the Jadester would soon be on their way to join us on the side of a Welsh mountain, Trix had been more cheerful. Girls like girl company – it's one of those strange things.

And you know what? Old Wik and I got caught up in the general feeling. When we got the call that the girls had arrived and were in the taxi from the station, we left our various tasks and went to a bank at the end of the long drive, which looked down the hill into the valley, to wait for the last two members of 'the gang' to arrive.

JADE

The English countryside: I don't get it. There's way too much weather. Everything's tiny – the roads, the shops, the people. The facilities are zilch. OK, I admit there are birds and trees and stuff and, if you happen to be one of those people who gets excited by birds and trees and stuff, there's no limit to the number of hours you can spend looking at them on account of their being everywhere all the time. For anyone else (i.e. anyone with a brain), the countryside is like school detention with scenery. I never saw the point of it.

So the news that we were now leaving a perfectly acceptable luxury villa to go to Wales, which I just knew was going to be even worse than English countryside, made my spirits sag big time.

OK, I thought, so we've got a self-kidnapping situation. We've got a lost summer holiday situation. What could possibly make the whole thing just that bit worse? Yup, that's right. A Welsh situation.

HOLLY

The taxi climbed and climbed. We left this little country road and went up a bumpy track. After about five minutes, we saw these scruffy village children ahead of us, sitting around doing nothing.

'Sheesh, meet the neighbours,' Jade said gloomily.

The taxi was about to pass them when the smallest of them started waving.

'That's not village children,' I said. 'That's them!'

And it was. Trix was actually jumping up and down as if she were a little kid.

We told the taxi-driver that we were fine here and paid him his fare. As we stepped out, we got our first proper view of Trix, Mark and Wiki.

They looked, well, different.

Jade stared at them as she stood by the taxi.

'What *happened* to you guys?' she said.

You know the cover of that book *Lord of the Flies*, the one where these kids hide up and take over this island or something? The children are all ragged, with dirty faces and a kind of crazed-animal look to them? That was Trix and the boys that day.

'You look like savages,' said Holly.

Trix hugged Holly and then me.

Mark made the usual grunting noise that passes for 'Hello, how are you?' in the world of boys.

'No offence and all that,' I said, 'but you guys look kind of revolting.'

Trix laughed. 'The whole washing thing is a bit less of a big deal here,' she said.

'We noticed,' said Holly.

Wiki picked up my suitcase, which I admit was rather large, and practically fell down the side of the hill. 'What have you got in here?' he asked.

'I like to accessorize,' I said. 'So kill me.'

He picked it up and smiled at me. Big admission: the countryside suited Wiki Church. He no longer looked as if you could sneeze him into the next county. He seemed to have grown some muscles in his arms. His spots had gone.

Then I saw it. I screamed. Something dead – a *creature* – was hanging from Wiki's belt.

'What is *that*? I asked, pointing with a trembling finger.

'Oh yeah, I forgot. I've got to skin that rabbit,' said Wiki.

'Oh, barf city,' I said. 'I *like* bunnies. Is it dead?'

'What do you think?' Mark was actually laughing.

Holly looked at the rabbit, then at Wiki.

'Did you just say "skin it"?'

That evening, the five of us sat in the attic ('Hey, a den, that is so cool,' said Jade), watching the early evening news.

Trix was the second story, after some big money crisis.

'The parents of missing teenager Trixie Bell are to turn to the leading publicist Eddison Vogel to help in the search for their daughter.' The newscaster managed to sound slightly surprised by this development. 'Here's our correspondent Fiona Maxwell.'

The woman who was reporting our case – Mark called her 'our Little Trixie Bell correspondent' – appeared on the screen.

For a change she was not outside Trix's house but in central London. She could tell us exclusively that the country's leading expert on publicity was to give his services free of charge to Eva Johansson and her husband, Jason Everleigh. She had spoken to him earlier in his office.

A small man with big hair sat behind a desk empty of paper. As he began to speak, his name 'Eddison Vogel' appeared at the bottom of the screen. In a soft voice, he said that like the rest of the nation he had been touched and moved by the story of little Trixie Bell. He had met Eva and Jason in the past. When Jason had asked whether he might be able to help, he had not hesitated before agreeing.

'This is not your normal type of business, Mr Vogel,' said Fiona.

'Because it's not business.' Vogel smiled, but there was just a hint of irritation. 'This is about looking out for each other. About caring for another human being.' He glanced at the camera as if suddenly noticing that an old friend was in the room. 'I can do a little bit. The people out there can do a little bit. This is all about working together to get little Trixie back to her family where she belongs. That's the thing – the only thing – that matters, Fiona.'

For a moment, the Trixie correspondent seemed too moved to speak. Then she returned us to the studio.

It was Trix who hit the Off button. 'What was all that about?' she said.

JASON EVERLEIGH

Let's get this straight. I have a heart as big as any man. You want tears. I can cry as much as anyone – maybe more. Just because I'm a successful businessman, it doesn't mean that I'm not into caring.

Trixie was my stepdaughter. Someone had taken her. My wife was in bits. I'd had to leave several important projects stateside on hold. I had the press camped on my doorstep. I had a policeman hanging around the place as if he were a member of the family.

It was a situation. Situations need problem-solvers.

So I had put in a call to the best problem-solver in the business, Eddison Vogel. Soon he was changing everything.

PETE BELL

When I was a journalist, Eddison Vogel was known as 'the Rodent'. He called himself a publicist, but whenever there was something nasty in the press – a big showbiz divorce, a politician behaving badly, some actor with a drink or drugs problem – the Rodent would soon be sniffing about.

I met him once. He didn't look like a rat – more like a sleek well-kept mouse, but one with a dangerous bite. He was small, elegantly dressed, with a neat beard and shiny, perfectly manicured nails. He smelt very expensive – the very best man-scents were fighting for attention on his neat little body.

He spoke very quietly in an accent that was slightly German, with a hint of Eastern Europe, all smoothed over by a smiling mid-Atlantic charm. No one knew where Vogel came from. Some said he was once a brilliant professor. Others that he wrote poetry in his spare time.

All I knew was that he gave me the creeps. There was something about Vogel that made me want to wash my hands after I had met him.

And now he had been brought in to help find my only child.

EDDISON VOGEL

We each of us have our own weaknesses. My personal weakness is that I am too nice. Not many people realize that. They think that Eddison Vogel is only interested in money and his famous friends. Not true. I have been lucky in my life. I like to give back. Ordinary people are important to me.

So a few days after agreeing to handle the public relations side of the Little Trixie Bell project, I gathered the key players at Eva Johansson's house and explained to them what I could bring to the party. No, scrub that. Put: what I could contribute in this tragic and difficult situation.

I had given the matter of Little Trixie Bell much thought. I had asked my researcher to come up with a campaign. That Sunday, in the conservatory at Jason and Eva's house, I presented it to the family and to Barry Cartwright.

I asked him where his investigation now stood.

'We have established various useful leads,' he said. 'There is the taxi-driver. Door-to-door interviews have been conducted in the neighbourhood of Little Trixie's home and we have also spoken to teachers at Cathcart College. We are convinced that she is still alive and that the trail is still warm.'

Barry spoke at some length. The more I heard, the more clearly I saw the situation. He was floundering. The police hadn't a clue what to do next.

'Excellent,' I said when at last he had droned to a halt. 'But let's come at this story from a different angle. We have to get the public involved. We have to make people care about Trixie Bell. They must feel involved – almost as if it is their own daughter, granddaughter, sister, friend who has disappeared. Once Trixie has a place in the heart of the nation, finding her will be only a matter of time.'

I paused, allowing my words to sink in. 'We have to develop a story – a narrative. What's the story with Trixie Bell?'

'She's a very caring girl,' said her mother.

'Caring? Great,' I said. 'Tell me more.'

WIKI

Everything was different after Holly and Jade arrived. It was as if they brought the Cathcart spirit to Hill Farm. I don't mean that in a good way.

Life in the country had changed Mark and me. The business of surviving had made him less cocky and me more confident. We didn't exactly like each other – he'd call me 'Speccy' now and then, and he liked to remind me that it was his godfather who had got the whole kidnap thing under way – but we kind of recognized we were in it together.

Soon Jade had changed too. She became more Jade. She decided that life in the country was gross, or a drag, or sometimes even Barf City.

She thought Gideon was creepy. She complained that there were no pizzas. If I have one memory of that week after the girls arrived, it is of Jade hanging around Trix and Holly, muttering about how her shoes were being ruined.

JADE

I had come to this crazy wilderness of a place, wearing shoes from Prada's spring collection. Big, big mistake. No one had mentioned that the Trix thing would involve my becoming a total fashion victim. I was the only person on

that farm who cared what they looked like, which meant
that in a real way I was suffering more than anyone else.

Not that I made a fuss about it.

MARK

Some gang. Most of us were keeping out of each other's
way. I was just beginning to wonder how we were going
to get the Trixter back home without getting into trouble
ourselves when things took a serious turn for the worst.

WIKI

We had this ritual. When Mark and I returned from the
shop with the day's papers, we would go to the attic
and check out how the Little Trixie investigation was
going.

That Sunday, the newspapers had a big front-page story
about her. It was headlined 'OUR LITTLE ANGEL'. There
was a new picture of Trix, wearing a Feed-the-World T-shirt.
Beneath it was written: 'Little Trixie Bell – all she wanted
was to save the lives of children.'

Inside there was a big profile under the heading 'SHE
CARED THAT WE DIDN'T CARE'. The newspaper had
talked to everyone – Trix's mum, her dad, Miss Fothergill,
even Griffo Griffiths.

Suddenly Trix was no longer just another kid. She was
like this walking conscience, 'the hidden face of our caring
teenagers'. There was the story of the fashion show at
Cathcart and how it had gone wrong, and a picture of her

room at school with all its photographs and posters about the starving in Africa.

I read it out to the others. At first we laughed – Trix was being described as a weird, perfect version of the Trix we knew.

'What's this got to do with my kidnapping?' Trix asked at one point.

I read the closing paragraph.

'Now, in a cruel twist of fate, Little Trixie Bell, the teenager who campaigned against cruelty and violence, is a victim of cruelty and violence herself. The last word should go to the man leading the hunt for the missing girl, Detective Inspector Barry Cartwright. "We owe it to our children to find this brave little girl who has shown us how to care. Each of us must do our part to make sure that Little Trixie is found and returned to her family."'

At the bottom of the page, it was announced that a Show Us You Care fund had been established. Readers were urged to 'do their bit. Every pound will help in the search for Trixie Bell'.

HOLLY

I expected Trix to be pleased. I mean, her plan had been to get the money rolling in. But she looked shocked, pale.

'Whoa,' said Jade, her usual tactful self. 'Saint Trix. Can I touch the hem of your garment?'

'It's sick,' said Trix. 'I don't know what we should do now.'

We sat in silence, looking at the newspaper spread all over the floor. Then, as if in answer to her question, my mobile rang. It was Mum, phoning from Italy.

'Holly, love,' she said, 'sorry to bother you but you have to come home. The police want to speak to you.'

WIKI

I needed to clear my head. There was too much stuff going on between the five of us. In the outside world the kidnap seemed to be slipping out of control.

The following afternoon I went for a walk to think about the next stage. I found my favourite spot – an old oak log overlooking the valley. I took out the knife Gideon had lent me and whittled at a Y-shaped ash branch I was making into the shape of a catapult. Here's how I saw the situation:

Reasons for continuing with the kidnap plan

1. I had promised Trix that I would help her.

2. We had managed to give the police the slip.

3. Living at Hill Farm had been the best fun I had ever had.

4. I don't like abandoning projects halfway through.

5. That's about it really.

Reasons for abandoning the kidnap plan
1. We had no idea what to do next.

2. Being at the centre of something that was on the front page of the newspapers was kind of scary.

3. Just because we were staying with his godfather, Mark suddenly seemed to assume he was in charge of things.

4. Gideon suspected something. I just knew it.

5. Holly reminded me of my life at Cathcart and looked at me as if I was some kind of sad case.

6. Jade was going to drive me clean up the wall.

7. I saw less of Trix now that the girls had arrived at the farm.

8. Why were we doing this? We must have been breaking about a million laws. Maybe it would have been better just to give some money to charity and have done with it.

9. I'd get expelled from Cathcart. The shock would kill my parents and I'd have to live the rest of my life with a cloud of guilt over my head.

10. I'd get found out. I always do. I'm just one of those people who get found out. It might be something in my genes.

11. 'You lied to us, William.' I can hear my mother saying that. 'How could you do such a thing?'

12. 'Because of Africa, Mum. Eighty-two point three per cent of the world's starvation is in that one continent.'

13. 'Don't try to blind me with science, William. Since when have you been interested in Africa? Is Africa worth destroying your education – your whole life – for?'

14. 'Well, William, is it?' Even Dad would turn on me. 'Answer your mother. And no lying this time.'

'Yes. I mean no. I don't know.' I spoke the words out loud and they hung in the hot summer air for a moment.

A twig snapped behind me. I was not alone. Surprised, embarrassed, I stood up.

It was Trix. She had been standing in the woods behind me.

'Easy, warrior,' she said, smiling.

I looked down and realized that I had a knife in one hand and a half-made catapult in the other.

She walked over to me. We sat on the log together.

'Your catapult's not going to work like that,' she said. 'It needs a bit of elastic between the two bits of wood. Just a hint.'

I laughed, turning the Y-shaped ash branch in my hand. 'It's kind of a work in progress,' I said.

We sat in silence for a few moments.

'You're different these days,' she said.

'Sorry about that.'

'No. It's good. When you came here, you were this geeky city boy. Now you're –' she laughed – 'you're almost tough.'

I shrugged and looked away.

'Yes, no, what?' she asked.

'Hm?'

'You were having a very serious conversation with yourself.'

'I was thinking about how all this was going.'

'Whether we should give up?'

I shrugged.

'Me too,' she said.

I looked at her, surprised. Trix is not exactly famous for changing her mind.

'It's going OK, but we can only do it if we work together,' she said. 'And right now I just can't see that happening. Mark's showing off. Holly's wishing she was on holiday. Jade's . . . Jade. Talk about an odd bunch.'

'D'you think the police are on to us? That that's why they want to talk to Holly?'

'No. Otherwise Jade would have had a call.'

'We could wait and see what they say to her.'

Trix shook her head. 'They'll tap her mobile. The way I see it, we've got a choice. We either get organized and push this thing through. We need to have a plan. Each of us has to play our part.'

'Or?'

'We go home. The rest of you can say you had no idea what was going on. I'll admit that I had some crazy plan. I've had a breakdown – what my dad calls a "teenage freak-out".'

'Adolescent pattern schizophrenia,' I murmured.

'Hm?'

'That would be the most likely type of teenage freak-out for you to be suffering from,' I explained. 'Adolescent pattern schizophrenia starts later usually – about seventeen or eighteen – but you could probably get away with it.'

Trix was looking at me. 'You are so weird, Wik,' she said.

'Just trying to be helpful,' I said.

'Anyway, whatever the teenage freak-out's called, everyone will be so pleased that I'm home, it'll soon be forgotten.'

'Little Trixie won't be an angel any more.'

Trix sighed. 'She never was. I'll be just another messed-up teenager making life difficult for adults.'

'The Trixter.'

'Right.' She smiled sadly, then took a photograph out of the back pocket of her trousers. It was a small, close-up photograph of an African child whose picture had been on the wall of her room at Cathcart. 'I just wanted to do something to help them,' she said, almost to herself.

'I don't mind getting into trouble,' I said. 'Maybe the other three will come through. We should give them the chance.'

Trix took the ash catapult from my hand and studied it carefully. 'It would be us against the adults.'

'We've done all right so far.'

'Luck,' she said. 'This is where it gets tough.'

I stood up. Something in our conversation had helped me make up my mind.

'The way I see it, we should just explain the situation to the others. I reckon if you and me are strong, we've got a chance of persuading them.'

A tense half-smile appeared on Trix's face when she was excited by something but was trying hard to be cool and grown up. 'You and me,' she said. 'You mean it?'

I nodded. 'I'm in. What do we do next?'

So, sitting there in the sun, we started to plan our next move.

JADE

Oh, great. I had blown my summer holiday. I was stuck in the wild Welsh mountains and now Holly was going to have to go home, leaving me with Nerdy Boy, Saint Trixie, Mark Bliss and his weirdo godfather.

Could things possibly get worse? Don't ask.

MARK

The atmosphere went into a major slump that day. Holly had been given one last day in the countryside and was due to return to London the next day. Jade spent most of the day sulkily leafing through the celebrity gossip in the papers, sighing now and then. Trix and Wiki had disappeared somewhere.

Me? I was getting bored. 'The Vanish' was becoming a serious drag. I thought about what my dad would do in this situation. He believes in doing stuff, keeping moving. 'Action, that's the thing, Mark,' he once told me. It's probably why he has to be abroad so much.

My father was out of contact, but I thought maybe a little chat with his former best friend might help. I went to see Gideon in his workshop. He sat at his bench, studying a bit of carved wood through his glasses as if it contained all the secrets of the universe.

'How's it going, Gideon?'

He shook his head, an irritated little frown on his face. Maybe it was the wood, maybe it was me. Either way, he was not in the mood for a chat with his godson.

I looked out of the window and saw Trix and Wiki

striding across the field towards the house, scattering hens as they went. They seemed to be in a hurry.

I made my way out to see what was up. As they approached, Wiki said, 'We're having a meeting. After supper.'

I shook my head. 'Enough for the moment, guys. Let's do it tomorrow.'

They just kept walking. 'In the attic,' Trix said. 'We need to talk to the whole gang today.'

I watched them as they entered the house.

Gang? I thought. *We?*

CHARLES 'THE SMILER' PRENDERGAST

Between you and me, I was overdue some luck. Eight years inside, a wife and kids who won't speak to me, a job (robbing post offices) that has very little security or long-term prospects.

All in all, the Smiler had very little to smile about.

Until . . . a rumour. A little birdie. Suddenly I was back in the big time with more job satisfaction than anyone could dream of.

And why? Because at last, after all these years, my luck turned.

If there's someone up there who looks after thieves, bank robbers and murderers and others who have strayed from the old straight and narrow, then I have two words for Him.

Thank you.

WIKI

In her citizenship classes at Cathcart College, Miss Fothergill now and then used to bring in a CD called *Great Speeches of the Twentieth Century*. Sometimes, she told us, it was not enough merely to be a good citizen. You had to persuade others to be good too.

She would put the CD in the classroom sound system and play us a few minutes of a speech from some twentieth-century guy who she said was one of our great role models. Sometimes it would be Sir Winston Churchill talking about the darkest hour and fighting on the beaches in the Second World War. Sometimes it was John F. Kennedy standing in front of the Berlin Wall. A particular favourite was Martin Luther King and his famous 'I have a dream' speech.

That evening after supper, as the light faded in the attic and we lit candles so that we could see what we were doing, Trix had her Churchill/Kennedy/King moment. She talked to us for maybe ten minutes and, with those few words, she changed everything.

HOLLY

There was a whiff of rebellion in the ranks that night. I was nervous about what I was going to say to the police the next day. Jade had had quite enough of the countryside. Mark had been moody ever since we had arrived.

Talking later, we discovered that each of us had pretty much the same idea in our head. It's over. The only question to decide was how exactly we were going to get Trix back home and keep ourselves out of trouble.

MARK

Don't get me wrong, but the little mini-gang of Wiki and the Trixter was beginning to get to me. Holly and Jade I didn't care about – they were girls and girls can do friendship as if it is natural. But I had been pretty much the main mover in this little plan. Where would we have been hiding out, for instance, it is were not for my godfather Gideon Burrowes?

But when things started getting tough, it was not me she turned to but one of the biggest dweebs, dorks and all-round speccy losers to go to Cathcart College – Wiki Church.

I didn't get it.

JADE

The attic: that night there was a semicircle of candles where we normally sat.

'Whoa, spooky,' I said as I reached the top of the ladder and poked my head through the trapdoor. 'Is this some kind of witches' coven?'

'Yeah.' Mark was sprawled on a huge cushion that he had found. He was wearing dark glasses for his own Markish reasons (I think he thought he looked cool. No, seriously). 'Maybe we're going to sacrifice a chicken or something.'

'Leave it out, Mark.' To my surprise, it was Wiki who spoke.

Mark turned to me. 'Hey, now I know who old Wik reminds me of,' he said. 'He's Harry Potter, only he's black and he's got a bit of a skin problem. That's it – he's Harry Spotter.'

I laughed. 'You're not a total zit-free zone yourself, frat boy.'

He winked at me as if he and I shared some kind of secret. I hate it when boys do that.

Holly's head appeared through the trapdoor.

'Boy, I'm going to miss all this when I get back to civilization,' she said, hauling herself up. '*Not!*'

She sat down opposite Mark and me. 'I hope this isn't going to take long. I've got to lie to the police tomorrow. I need a good night's sleep.'

Sheesh. I'm not exactly the most observant person in the world but even I could tell that the atmosphere that night was not the greatest.

WIKI

When Mark made his Harry Spotter joke, it was like a kick in the stomach. I had thought we were becoming friends. I was about to say something when Trix darted me a look.

I kept quiet. I gripped the catapult in my pocket and concentrated on the meeting. It wasn't easy.

Trix stood up. There was something about her, a sort of stillness, that wiped the smile off Mark's face, and made Holly and Jade pay attention. She picked up one of the newspapers that lay on the floor and looked at it, then around at each of us.

'They're setting up a fund – the Show Us You Care fund.' She spoke so quietly she might have been talking to herself. 'We've done OK. If we can get hold of the money it raises, we will already have saved hundreds, maybe thousands of lives.'

'Yeah. Big if,' muttered Jade.

'Not bad for five kids,' Trix continued, ignoring her. 'The question now is whether we go on. It's started well, our little plan, but from here it gets tougher. Let me tell you how I see it.'

She talked about The Vanish, the escape out of London, Gideon, Hill Farm, the arrival of Holly and Jade, the gang. The rest of us had become used to talking about what had happened as an adventure, almost a private joke, but the way Trix talked now, it was deadly serious.

This was our chance to do something, she said – to use the privilege we had enjoyed throughout our lives for something good in the world.

'If we stop now,' said Trix, 'this will be just one of those crazy rich-kid pranks. But if we go on—'

'It'll matter.' Holly was the one who spoke.

'Yes,' said Trix. 'It will really matter. We can change things.'

No one was smiling now. Something else, a strange and powerful new spirit, had suddenly kicked in. My mouth was dry. My heart thumped. I willed Trix to keep talking, to tell us what we should do.

But it was at that moment, when she had won us over, that she turned the decision over to us.

'Kids,' she said quietly. 'That's what they call us. You remember one of the newspaper reports said, "Kids get up to all sorts of things that their parents know nothing about." As if adults have made such a great job of the world. I thought, just maybe, we are in a position to show them

136

what kids can do – even when the whole grown-up world is against them.'

'Kids against adults,' murmured Mark.

'The choice is yours.' Trix was almost whispering now, her dark eyes glittering, her pale face lit by the candlelight. 'I know where I stand. But I can't do it alone. So we leave it here or we go on together. What do you think?'

I was about to speak up, but swallowed my words and kept quiet. I realized, just in time, that my support was not exactly going to encourage Mark, and maybe even the others, to join in.

'I'm in,' said Holly. 'I haven't done much so far.'

Mark shrugged, trying to seem cool. 'You've convinced me, Trixter, ' he said. 'I'm up for anything.'

We looked at Jade, who sat wide-eyed and pale. If she had been anyone else, I would have thought she was lost in thought.

'Heavee,' she said eventually.

No one laughed. Jade cleared her throat like someone about to make a very important announcement. 'Straight from the shoulder, right?' she said. 'This was all majorly Holly's idea. I kind of came along for the ride. If you want the honest truth as to whether I'd rather be hanging out with Mark's hobo godfather in Wales or by a pool in Italy, well, I guess you know the answer.'

'Jade, if you go back home, the whole thing's over,' said Holly.

'I know that, you dork!' Jade snapped. 'And that's not why I'm staying – as if I cared what you guys really think. I so do not.' She paused for a moment. 'There's family stuff. I've been thinking about it since I've been up here in this hellhole. What Trix said just then kind of spoke to me.'

She nodded, almost like a little kid. 'Yup, yup, yup. I'm in. Jade's in.'

Again I thought it was my moment, but Trix spoke next.

'Wiki's in,' she said in a matter-of-fact voice. 'He'll be doing the planning with me.'

Three pairs of eyes turned in my direction. None of them friendly.

'Anyone got a problem with that?' Trix asked. Silence. 'Great,' she said. 'So the first thing we need to know is what we're each good at.'

'How do you mean?' asked Holly.

'We want to get a million pounds to Africa,' said Trix. 'It's not strictly legal what we're doing. Some people would say it's a major crime. So we need to see what skills we have.'

THE SMILER

You'll be wondering about my name. People do. The world calls me Charles (or maybe Charlie) Prendergast. My friends, people in my line of business (crime), know me as 'The Smiler'.

If you could see me now, you would know the reason. Down the right side of my face is this scar, five and a half inches from the top of my ear to the side of my mouth. Some people might find it unsightly, although they never say so to my face. Personally, I think it gives me a character, a bit of warmth, on account of it making me look at first glance as if I'm smiling.

How did it happen? A bit of silliness a long time ago when

I was seventeen. Saturday night. Pub. Drink. Someone said something I wasn't too happy with. We stepped outside to sort it out. I ended up with a bit of damage to my face – the sort of damage that lasts a lifetime. He didn't look too clever either, after I had finished with him.

At least I got a name out of it. I like being one of life's smilers. You know what they say – smile and the world smiles with you. Hasn't happened to me yet – nobody smiles when I'm around, for some reason – but hope springs eternal. I never saw myself as a Charles, as it happens.

But then I never saw myself at the age of fifty-five, in my prime, living in Wales, robbing the odd village post office to keep body and soul together.

I'm quite bitter about that, to tell the truth. It all goes back to a job I did sixteen years ago. There was this bank. It got itself done over. By me, as it happens. Some idiot had seen too many films and tried to be a hero. Bad idea. He ended up in hospital with a rather nasty bump on the head. He'll never be quite the same again, they say.

Apart from that little detail, the story would have ended happily. The gang got away with the cash. The police were safely paid off. It all would have been fine if a journalist hadn't allowed his curiosity to get the better of him.

Quite the little Sherlock Holmes he was. Thanks to him, I spent eight years inside. When I came out, no one in the business (crime) wanted to know me. Not even my own flesh and blood.

'Lay low for a while,' I was told. Low? I went high into the Welsh mountains, where a man can buy a house for cash, no questions asked.

For a year, I waited for my luck to change. Then one day it did.

The moment had come. The moment when the Smiler could get his revenge at last.

That Sherlock Holmes journalist. Maybe you've heard his name mentioned.

Mr Peter Bell.

WIKI

It's not a question you get asked every day: you are about to commit the crime of the century. What skill will you be able to offer?

'You don't have to be great at things,' Trix said, filling in the silence. 'We're not talking genius here.'

I looked at Holly, Jade and Mark. Their faces were blank. It was not a great start.

'Mark.' I stepped forward and stood beside Trix. 'You're good with cars, aren't you?'

He shrugged. 'I know my way round an engine.'

'Can you drive?' Jade asked.

'Of course I can drive. My dad says I'm a better driver than most adults. I've got an uncle who used to work in Grand Prix racing. I've driven at eighty miles per hour round a racetrack.'

'Ooooh.' Jade made a little mocking noise. No one laughed.

Trix smiled. 'That could be useful for a start. Anyone else?'

'I can speak French and Italian,' said Holly. 'But I'm not going to be with you guys, am I?'

'You can do voices too,' said Jade.

Holly smiled. 'Oh terrific, yeah, I so majorly can.' The voice was Jade's to perfection.

'That's amazing,' said Mark. 'Can you do me?'

'Hey, babester –' Holly dropped her voice and spoke huskily – 'I'm Mark Bliss, hanging out with the guys, right? The Trixter? The Wikster? The Jadester? You can call me the Blisster.'

We all laughed.

'Wiki? What can you do?' Trix turned to me.

I winced. 'I'm good at computers.'

'Nerdy Boy,' muttered Mark.

'I'm OK generally with technical stuff. I can hack into most programmes.'

'And you're a pretty good shot with a gun,' said Mark. 'I hate to admit it but you have a good eye.'

I took the catapult out of my back pocket. That morning Gideon had helped me fix a heavy elastic sling to the ash fork I had been whittling. It was a great weapon. 'I prefer this,' I said.

'I don't know if it will help but I have loads of celebrity contacts,' said Trix. 'And I know how the charity business works. Oh, and I know newspaper people through my dad.'

'We're getting somewhere,' said Holly. 'Cars, computers, friends in high places, silly voices.'

'We've pulled off a fake kidnap,' said Trix. 'Now we've got to stay in hiding until there's enough money in the rescue fund to make a difference in Africa. Then get our hands on the cash.'

There was a small, actressy sniff from the direction of Jade.

'What about you, Jade?' Trix asked quietly. 'Do you have any skills that might be useful?'

'Maybe I should just go home now.' When she spoke,

Jade sounded tearful. 'You're all such geniuses, aren't you? Face it, I've got nothing to offer.'

There was an awkward silence as each of us racked our brains to think of a talent – any talent – that Jade might have.

Nada, as she might say.

'See?' said Jade. 'It's embarrassing. I'm useless.'

A thought occurred to me. 'You're good at being the centre of attention,' I said.

'Gee, thanks, Wiki,' said Jade sourly. 'You really know how to help a girl deal with her self-esteem issues.'

'I'm not joking,' I said. 'When you're around, everyone looks at you. Hasn't anyone noticed that?'

'Suppose so,' Holly muttered. 'It's what I hate about her most. When I take her home, I'm suddenly invisible. It's all, "What does Jade want?" and "What do you think, Jade?" They never ask me that. And they're meant to be my parents.'

'They're just being polite, you goof.' Suddenly Jade's spirits seemed to have revived. 'Nobody's that interested in me.' She looked around, all wide-eyed. 'Are they?'

'That's another thing you're good at.' This was Mark. 'Pretending to be innocent. I think you're the best liar I've ever met.'

'Excuse me.' Jade sat up angrily. 'I didn't come here to be—'

'What about contacts?' Trix asked. 'Do you know anyone who could help us? What about your brothers?'

Jade looked away. 'You don't want to know about them,' she said. 'They're totally bad news.'

Trix was about to press her, but Holly caught her eye and shook her head slowly. Jade's family, it seemed, was a no-go area.

JADE

Perfecto. Here were the skills that I was going to bring to the party: showing off and lying. Then there was that question about my contacts. This is what I should have said when they brought my so-called family into the discussion: Hey, guys, rearrange the following words to make a famous phrase or saying: 'go', ' there' and 'don't'.

THE SMILER

I like to have contacts. People who tell me stuff. One of my best contacts is a little guy called Spider Webb. Spider's not the sharpest tool in the shed, never having got around to reading or writing, but he's bright enough to do the rounds collecting scrap from remote houses and doing a spot of light thieving now and then to keep him in beer money.

Chatting with me in the pub one night, he mentioned this weirdo Gideon. Lived alone, apparently. Except now he had five children running around the place. What was odd was that, when Spider had called by unannounced, the children had seemed nervous about him seeing them.

This Gideon bloke was a strange one, according to Spider. Long-haired hippy type. Drove around in a London taxi.

Somewhere, deep in the Smiler bonce, bells were beginning to ring.

'Tell me about the kids,' I said. 'What did they look like?'

EVA JOHANSSON

Eddison is a genius. The weekend newspaper stories about Trixie's passion for justice in the world changed everything. It was as if they had been waiting to find out whether she was a good teenager or a bad teenager. If she had run off with someone she had met on an Internet chatline (which I never believed), then she was not worth quite the fuss in the newspapers.

Now, thanks to Eddison Vogel, they understood my little Trixie. She was a good, caring girl. An angel.

A genuine twenty-first-century child heroine.

EDDISON VOGEL

We had lift-off. The Little Trixie story had it all. There were glamorous parents with a little bit of sad family history, thanks to Pete, the alcoholic father. There was money, privilege and famous friends. There was a detective who looked good in front of the cameras and enjoying playing the part. And then there was Little Trixie herself, the teenager who cared that we didn't care.

A whole guilt thing kicked in beautifully. It gave the story what I like to call 'traction' – something ordinary folk can relate to. Thanks to Trixie, millions of people would start thinking about their own lives – how selfish they were, how little they thought about the starving kids in the world. They would compare themselves to this innocent little fourteen-year-old. The idea would take hold that somehow the big, uncaring world – that's you and me, folks – was somehow responsible for what had happened to Trixie. Then the money would start pouring into the Show Us You Care fund, and that would help the story along too. The public likes to be reminded of how big-hearted it can be.

Newspapers were already desperately looking for new angles. When I told them that Trixie's best friend might be available for interview, I almost had a riot on my hands.

I just hoped this Holly kid would play her part. The child element – that was what we wanted. It was going to be a real heartbreaker.

DETECTIVE INSPECTOR BARRY CARTWRIGHT

Some investigations are straightforward. There's a crime, there's a criminal out there and there's evidence. My job is to bring those things together in a way that will satisfy a court of law. The investigation begins and ends with the police.

Then there are the complicated ones. Once in a while there are cases that 'catch fire', as we policemen like to say. Everyone's interested. The crime is a story in which the public is determined to play its part.

The disappearance of Little Trixie Bell was one of those.

As the officer responsible for the investigation, I was at first keen to keep the journalists, the television cameras, away from the case. Crime-solving is like managing the national football team – everyone thinks he can do it better than the experts.

Me, I can do without the amateurs. They think they're the famous continental detective Hercule Poirot when in fact they're the famous continental idiot Inspector Clouseau.

When Eddison Vogel was brought in by Eva Johansson, he made me see things differently. The public, he said, doesn't have to be the enemy. It can be your friend.

'We've got to keep them interested,' he said. 'There's always another big human-interest story around the corner.'

PETE BELL

Have you tried to give up drink? It's not easy. Since the day after Trix had disappeared, I hadn't touched a drop. My body did not like what was happening to it. I lost weight. My hands shook. I looked – well, I looked worse than when I was drinking.

No one knew I was dry, of course. My ex-wife continued to look at me as if a bit of dog-do had just walked into her house. She still referred to me, even when I was in hearing range, as 'the Drunk'.

MARK

We had told Gideon that Holly was having to return for a family wedding. While he was taking Holly to the station after breakfast, Wiki and I cycled to the shop during the morning to pick up the papers and the shopping for the day.

To tell the truth, I had a small twinge of worry as we

cycled off, leaving Trix and Jade alone at Hill Farm. Maybe all the talk of crimes and plans the previous evening was getting to me.

THE SMILER

You'll want to know my plan.

It was simple. For some reason, Pete Bell's kid was being held by the taxi-driving hippy Gideon.

No one in the world knew this except the Smiler.

I would check out the house. The next day I would grab the kid, hold on to her long enough to make Pete Bell suffer like I suffered in jail. Then I would give her back – in return for a few thousand pounds.

Revenge and cash. It was beautiful.

JADE

Maybe you've picked up on this already: Jade Hart is not a country girl. When it was decided over breakfast that Trix and I were going to be picking berries while Holly went to the station and the boys did the shopping, my first thought had been: I want to go back to bed.

But I didn't because that's the kind of girl I am – a team player.

THE SMILER

The taxi rumbled down the driveway to the small country

lane leading down to the main road. From my Discovery, which I had parked out of sight up a lane, I caught a glimpse of Gideon as he drove past. There was a small figure in the back of the car. Little Trixie? Probably. Wherever he was taking her, I sure as hell hoped he would be bringing her back.

One minute, two. I slipped on my trusty leather gloves, turned the key in the Discovery and eased out of the lane and up the hill. I was on my way.

JADE

The sun shone. The birds sang. Trix was up a plum tree and I was down among the gooseberries, getting pricked to hell.

We had been working about five minutes when we heard the taxi coming back.

Except it wasn't the taxi. A big black SUV with darkened windows was moving towards us up the drive. There was something about the way it was being driven – slowly, quietly, like some beast stalking its prey – that gave me a bad, bad feeling.

'OK.' Trix spoke quietly. 'We just stay here very quietly, right, Jade. Keep out of sight.'

Like I needed encouraging.

The SUV turned in front of the house until it was facing down the hill again. A man stepped out. He wore a sky-blue tracksuit and trainers – not a good look, I remember thinking, for a man whose hair was grey and who had a paunch like he was about six months pregnant. Weirdest of all, he had on these black leather gloves.

He walked to the front door, which was open as usual:
knocked and waited. After about thirty seconds, he walked
into the kitchen.

THE SMILER

Something a bit iffy was going on here. Trust me. I've got a
nose for these things.

This farm was too normal.

I've never kidnapped anyone myself (although, come
to think of it, I did once lock a bank manager's wife in
a lavatory for about six hours), but I'm pretty sure that
kidnappers don't leave the front door open. And there's
probably not the smell of baking bread in the average
snatcher's hideout.

Not my problem. Whatever the story, the world –
including my enemy, the toerag Pete Bell – thought that
this girl Trixie had been kidnapped. That was all that
mattered.

I went upstairs. There was kids' stuff everywhere. The
first bedroom I went into was used by boys, to judge by the
mess. Next door, it was neater. I was getting somewhere.
Beside one of the beds was a framed photograph – some
blonde chick, whose face I recognized. It was Eva
Johansson, when she was younger. Standing beside her, a
stupid grin on his silly face, was Bell.

Bingo. I opened the top drawer in the table. Some
clothes. I took out a small T-shirt. Written on it were the
words FEED THE WORLD. I stuffed it in my pocket and
went downstairs.

JADE

The man was inside the house for a couple of minutes. Trix and I watched, hardly daring to breathe, as he stood, framed by the front door.

That face. I'll never forget it. The eyes were cold, alert and, as he looked about him, he had this big scary grin on his face. At one point, he seemed to be gazing down to the orchard.

Don't scream, Jade. And please don't wet yourself.

He went round the back of the house.

THE SMILER

I was done. On an impulse, I checked out the yard, looked into one of the sheds. There were rocking chairs everywhere. On a table in the centre of the workshop there was a big chair someone had almost finished. I ran my hand over the wood. It was a beauty – the ultimate rocker.

A carpenter-kidnapper? This was one weird situation.

JADE

Walking quickly now, the man returned to his car, still grinning like a psycho. He gunned its engine and took off.

Silence. I looked at Trix. She looked at me. We were both too freaked to move or say anything.

That's how we were when Wiki and Mark appeared on their bikes about five minutes later.

WIKI

We called for the girls outside, then in the house. We went down to the orchard.

'Maybe they went for a walk,' Mark was saying.

'Jade? Walking?' I said. 'That'll be the day.'

As I spoke, there was a sound – a sort of whimper – from the gooseberry patch. She stood up. Even with her Italian tan, she looked pale.

'Jade,' I said. 'What is it?'

That was when she started crying.

MARK

Don't you hate it when girls fall apart? Seeing Jade cry like that, I was reminded of what my dad used to say when I was younger. Spare us the waterworks.

Jade was gabbling something about a psycho, a car. 'He was grinning, like he'd been told this big joke,' she said.

'Where's Trix?' Wiki asked.

'I'm here.'

The voice came from the branches of a tree behind us. Trix jumped down and, glancing nervously towards the drive, she said, 'We've had a visitor.'

The full story came out. At some point, Jade became hysterical, as if there was all this fear inside her that suddenly had to come pouring out.

The three of us looked at her, not sure what to do.

To my surprise, it was Wik who acted first. He moved towards her and put an arm round her shoulders.

'Don't, you dork!' Jade yelped, trying to wriggle away. But Wiki held her fast.

'You're OK,' he said. 'Everything is fine now.'

Slowly she calmed down.

'What happens if he comes back?' Trix asked.

'Maybe he was just a friend of Gideon's,' I said.

'Get real,' Jade snapped. 'Gideon doesn't have friends.'

'Here's what we do.' Wiki took his arm away from Jade. 'We go to the attic and decide on a plan.'

JADE

OK, so I lost it for a few moments there. But face it, we were all scared. At least I had the courage to show my feelings.

I got over it soon enough. The psycho was scary, sure, but having Wiki Church put his arm round me put things in perspective. That was even scarier.

In the attic, we had this big gang meeting and discussed what we should do next. Talk to Gideon? Get the hell out of there? Give ourselves up?

WIKI

It was the first real test for the gang since the big meeting the previous night, and it was not going well.

Mark and Jade agreed with one another for the first time in living history. We should tell Gideon about the visitor, they said. Trix pointed out that, if he called the police, it would be the end of everything.

'The police?' Mark laughed. 'My godfather would never

call the police. Anyway, he might know the guy. My dad says that when in doubt—'

'Well, your dad's not here, is he?' Trix snapped. She shook her head. 'I'm sorry, Mark. It's getting to me, all this.'

Mark gave an angry little shrug. He reached for one of the newspapers we had bought in the village and opened it. There was a big headline across two pages: 'THE TROUBLED LIFE OF LITTLE TRIXIE'S FATHER'. A big photograph showed a man who was unshaven and badly dressed. He looked like a beggar on a street corner. It was Pete Bell.

'That's an old picture,' said Trix. 'He doesn't look like that most of the time.'

Mark was reading the article. 'Hey, it says your dad was once the country's leading crime reporter,' he said. 'I never knew he had been famous.'

Trix said nothing. She was staring at the bottom of the page as if it she had seen something unspeakably terrifying.

'Jade,' she whispered, then pointed at a small photograph.

Jade looked down at the paper and screamed.

JADE

It was him. Oh my God. The psycho. The hair was longer, the face younger, but there was no mistaking that grin.

'Charles 'the Smiler' Prendergast', the caption read. 'Once Britain's most wanted man, Prendergast was jailed as a result of Bell's investigation. He was released from prison last year, having served eight years for robbery with violence.'

THE SMILER

As soon as I got home, I took a closer look at the T-shirt. Carefully – I didn't want any telltale Smiler DNA to slip through – I made a few cuts with some scissors into the material. Then I popped it into the post, addressed to the Show Us You Care fund address.

I'd have given anything to see Bell's face when it arrived.

WIKI

We had to get out of there, and fast. Even in those panicky moments, the thought made me sad. I liked these fields, these animals, these birds. It felt like home here.

Later that morning, waiting for Gideon to return from the station, I sat on my favourite log, looking out over the valley, thinking of my time at Hill Farm.

At one point, Jade joined me.

'Thanks for all that earlier,' she said.

I frowned, unsure of what she was talking about.

'In the orchard. I kind of lost it back there. You were, you know, OK.'

I smiled. 'You're welcome, Jade.'

'Just don't do it again, right?' she said, and began walking back to the house.

GODFATHER GIDEON

Humans are trouble. I prefer cats or hens or even foxes. Let humans too close to you and soon enough you'll regret it.

I had thought small humans, or 'children' as they're sometimes called, would mean less trouble. I was wrong.

Ever since the two girls had arrived, I had realized that there was more to this holiday than met the eye. There was too much whispering, too many meaningful glances across the table at mealtimes. Whatever their game was, I wanted nothing to do with it. I had work to do, a life to lead.

On the way to the station, the girl Holly had chattered away like a sparrow in spring. It was too much noise, too many words, so that after a while I said to her, 'You don't have to talk, you know. Enjoy the scenery.'

'Oh,' she said, a bit put out. 'Fine, right.' She remained silent until we said goodbye at the station. As we stood by the taxi, she stuck out her hand and said, with the good manners of a performing dog, 'Goodbye, Gideon, and thank you for having me to stay.'

I nodded.

Then she said, 'One day, you'll know how important it was.' With a wave, she was gone.

Yes, the children had a secret that was more than just a kids' game. I really didn't want to get involved.

Some hope.

WIKI

We went to see Godfather Gideon late that morning.

'Gideon.' Mark was our spokesman. 'There's something we need to tell you.'

'Noooo.' It was a long groan. Gideon ran his hands over the smooth wood of the rocking chair on the workbench in front of him. 'Not now.'

'But Gideon—' said Mark.

'Three months I've been working on this rocker based on a Shaker design. It's made from black walnut. There's nothing like this in the world.'

'How much will it go for?' asked Jade.

'No idea,' said Gideon. 'The gallery sorts that out for me. The money is not important.' He gazed, smiling, at the chair, a sparkle of pride in his eyes. 'It's the work that matters. So –' He picked up a corner of sandpaper – 'if you don't mind, our chat can wait until tomorrow. I'm sure it's very interesting but—'

'I'm afraid we can't do that.' Trix stepped forward. 'This is too urgent to wait.'

GODFATHER GIDEON

And so the nightmare began.

At first as the children began to tell that story, I responded with the odd groan of despair. Charity. Africa. Decided to take action. Kidnap (GROAN). Escaped to Wales. Demon Taxi-Driver. (GROAN). Front-page head-lines.

But then, when they told me about the visitor in the 4x4 with blacked-out windows, I moved beyond groans. I buried my face in my hands. Why had I ever agreed to see these children?

156

'Sorry, Gideon.' My godson sounded unusually embarrassed. 'It's all got a bit out of hand, hasn't it?'

I sighed. 'You could say.'

WIKI

He didn't take it well. We were used to Gideon looking through us – the longer we stayed there, the less he seemed to see us. Now, though, it was as if the full horror of our presence had suddenly become clear to him.

'We'll go tomorrow,' Trix was saying. 'And this afternoon one of us will keep guard at the end of the drive. If this man Prendergast returns, the lookout will ring the house and we'll disappear to the attic.'

'As from tomorrow, it will be as if we'd never been here,' said Mark. 'If he turns up, you can say, "Trix? What Trix?"'

Muttering miserably to himself, Gideon started sanding an arm of the rocking chair. We filed out in silence.

'Well, that went really well, I must say,' said Jade, always the first to come up with the unhelpful comment.

JADE

No way was I doing the lookout thing. Sorry, guys, I do not want to see the Grinning Psycho again, least of all on my own.

So Wiki went first. Trix did the next two hours. It was during Mark's watch that it all happened.

MARK

I had been sitting under a tree. It was late afternoon but the sun was still hot. I was feeling sleepy. I was gazing, totally bored, down into the valley when I saw something move. A big 4x4 was heading slowly up the hill in our direction.

Our friend was back. I rang Jade's phone.

'He's on his way. Get up to the attic, now.'

Two minutes later, the vehicle, a Discovery, turned into the drive. It drove past me, accelerating up the hill, kicking up stones.

THE SMILER

This time I meant business. I had some rope for the kid, a baseball bat for security.

As I drove up, the place was quiet but the old London taxi was there. I stepped out. The door was shut this time. I knocked.

Nothing. Quietly I entered. There was no one in the house, downstairs or upstairs. It was when I was climbing the stairs that I heard a knocking sound.

Downstairs. Outside. Round the back. Into the shed. I didn't knock.

An old hippy was tapping at the rocking chair I had seen before. He was in a world of his own. So much so that I had to clear my throat.

He straightened up slowly and looked at me.

GODFATHER GIDEON

He was an ugly brute – short, thickset and with this strange smile on his face which I soon realized was not a smile at all, but some sort of old wound.

'Can I help you?' I asked.

'Where's Little Trixie?'

'I'm sorry, but I have no idea what you're talking about. Are you sure you have the right address?'

'Where is she? The kid? I know you've got her. I don't care what your game is. Just hand her over.'

He walked slowly towards me with the rolling gait of a retired boxer.

'I have never met a Little Trixie,' I said calmly.

He stood so close to me that I could smell the stale sweat on him.

THE SMILER

I don't like people who take advantage of my good nature. I really don't. It makes me want to persuade them to behave themselves.

GODFATHER GIDEON

The thug picked up a pair of pliers that were on the workbench. He tapped the black walnut rocker with it. 'Nice piece of work that,' he said in a low, husky voice.

'Please,' I said. 'Just leave the chair alone. It's quite . . . delicate.'

'I bet it is.' He put the pliers around one of the struts holding the back in place. I saw the muscles in his arm tense.

'Where's Trixie?' he asked.

I shook my head, unable to take my eyes away from where the pliers were turning harder and harder against the wood.

'Good workmanship,' said the thug. 'Not easy to break.'

There was a crack and I confess I gave a little gasp as if it were one of my own limbs that was being broken.

'There we go,' he said. 'It's like any work, the first bit's the hardest. The rest is going to be easy.'

He placed the pliers around another of the struts.

'Where is she?' he whispered.

'I don't know,' I said. 'Please don't destroy the chair. It's special – special to me.'

He shook his head. 'You're a very stupid man,' he said, turning the pliers once more. 'You're going to tell me in the end but by then this lovely chair will be firewood. Here we go again.'

He tightened his grip harder and harder. Suddenly there was a loud crack – only this time the noise came not from the chair but from the thug's head.

I looked into his eyes. They seemed to be fixed on something on the ceiling. Then they closed. Then his legs buckled and he fell to the floor.

I looked beyond where he lay, through the open door, into the yard.

Wiki stood there, his arms hanging by his sides. Dangling from his left hand was his catapult.

JADE

The five of us had been watching from the attic window. We could see little through the open doorway of the shed, but the voices reached us, first quiet, then threatening, rising. At one point, Gideon shouted, 'No!' and there was a loud crack of breaking wood.

It was then that the world's most unlikely boy hero went into action.

'Wik, wait,' Trix whispered, but Wiki was gone.

We saw him walking quickly but quietly out of the house. Halfway to the shed, he stopped, picked up a stone, put it in his catapult, aimed – and let fly.

Through the lit door of Gideon's workshop, something moved, then was silent.

Wiki walked slowly towards the shed.

WIKI

'He's not dead.' Gideon was crouching beside the man, his hand on his neck. 'The pulse is fine.'

He stood up slowly and reached out, like a man in a trance, for the rocking chair.

For a moment, I looked at the man's face. Knocked out cold, he no longer looked like he was smiling, but the scar was unmistakable. It was the man whose face was in the papers – Prendergast. A thin trickle of blood from his head was forming a puddle on the wooden floor.

'Maybe we should tie him up or something,' I said. 'When he comes round, he's not going to be too happy.'

'Yes.' Gideon reached inside a cupboard on the wall and took out some thick tape.

Together we turned Prendergast and I began to tape his wrists together.

Mark arrived, followed by Trix and Jade.

'I said no violence,' said Trix.

'Where did you learn to shoot like that?' asked Mark.

'I want my mom,' whispered Jade.

I looked at Trix. 'He was the one being violent,' I said quietly. I nodded in the direction of Gideon, who had returned to his rocking chair to inspect the damage.

'That's a chair, a thing. He's a –' Trix looked down at the scarred man – 'He's a . . .' She seemed to lose her drift for a moment.

'Human?' I said. 'I wouldn't count on it.' I began taping the man's feet together.

'Your lock-up shed, Gideon,' said Mark. 'Maybe we should put him in there before he wakes up.'

'Hm?' Gideon looked slowly at his godson. 'Oh, yeah, right. I'll get the key.' He walked towards the house.

'He's in shock,' said Mark. 'I've never seen him like this.'

'I've had enough of this nightmare now,' said Jade, still staring at the body on the floor. 'I'd like to wake up, please.'

'She's right,' said Mark. 'We should just call the police and turn ourselves in.'

'And all this will have been for nothing,' said Trix. 'We can't do that.'

I thought hard. 'We lock this guy in the shed. We get the hell out of here. Then Gideon can call the police. We'll ask him to keep quiet about us.'

'But where can we go?' asked Mark.

There was a moment's silence.

'I guess I could call my brothers,' Jade said suddenly.

'Your brothers?' said Trix. 'I thought –' She hesitated – 'Wasn't there some kind of trouble there?'

'Trouble? That word could have been invented for my brothers,' said Jade quietly. 'But we're desperate, right?'

'And how exactly are we going to get anywhere?' asked Mark.

I had thought of that. I crouched beside Prendergast and reached into a pocket of his tracksuit. I took out his keys and handed them to Mark.

'Maybe we should drive,' I said.

GODFATHER GIDEON

I wanted the children gone. I wanted everyone gone. I wanted my good and simple life back.

With the two boys, I dragged the scarred man to the tractor shed. It was reasonably secure. We locked it and returned to the kitchen.

'Gideon, we're packing and going.' My godson Mark spoke to me slowly as if I were some kind of moron. 'When we're on our way, go to the police. Tell them you've had an intruder. And – would it be possible? – don't mention us.'

JADE

I never thought that I would actually be glad to hear the voice of my older brother Brad on the phone.

'Brad,' I said. 'It's Jade. I'm in trouble. I need your help.'

'Shoot, babe.' (This is the way Brad talks.)

'I need you to meet me and some friends. Can we stay in the apartment?'

'It's kinda scuzzy right now, sis.'

Now there was a surprise. 'That's not a problem. Brad, get in the car and start driving.'

'Whoa, sis. And where exactly am I going?'

'Wales,' I said.

'*Wales?*'

HOLLY

I felt alone that first evening back home.

From the moment I had arrived back in London, there had been surprises. As I walked through the ticket barrier at the station, I had noticed that a gaggle of press photographers were snapping some celebrity nearby.

Then I noticed the celebrity was my mum. She was standing beside a tall woman dressed in black, who I recognized as Trix's mother Eva Johansson. Standing slightly aside from them was a small man with carefully combed hair.

'Holly! Darling!' My mother spotted me and, like some weird circus act, the posse of photographers wheeled around, faced me, and let off about a million flashes in my face.

My mother hugged me, flash, flash.

Trix's mum (a complete stranger to me) kissed me on both cheeks, flash, flash. The miniature man with the hair extended a hand.

164

'Holly de Vriess, the famous friend,' he said. 'It's a pleasure to meet you at last. My name is Eddison Vogel.'

I looked around, bewildered. 'Why are all these photographers here?'

The man smiled. 'We'll explain all that later. First you need to talk to the police. Then we've arranged a couple of little interviews with our favourite writers.'

'Interviews? With me?'

'"Tragic Trixie's closest friend", "The Trixie Bell I knew", that sort of thing,' said Eddison Vogel.

'But—'

'Just be yourself.' Vogel gave a creepy smile. 'And leave the rest to me.'

Be myself. It was the one thing that was impossible. In my room that night, I wondered what the gang would be doing now up in the hills with Godfather Gideon.

WIKI

We needed to get out of there. The four of us threw our bags on to the back seat. We ran back to Gideon, who was still sitting in his kitchen.

'Can you give us five minutes before you call the police, Gideon?' Trix asked.

He nodded.

'Thanks, Gid.' Jade kissed him on the cheek. He looked surprised. Wincing, Trix did the same. Mark patted him awkwardly on the back of his shoulders. 'You're a great godfather,' he said.

I held out my hand. 'Thank you, Gideon,' I said quietly.

He looked at me and, to my surprise, he smiled. 'You look after yourself, Wiki. Come and see me again when your stunt is over, right?'

I nodded.

We returned to the Discovery. 'Mark, are you sure you know how to drive this?' asked Jade.

'Watch me,' said Mark. He climbed into the driver's seat, put the key in and started the engine.

THE SMILER

Hm? Hmmm? HMMM! I awoke in darkness. There was a smell of oil and diesel. My head throbbed. It felt as if someone was in there, hammering against my brain to get out. My hands were taped. I tugged and pulled until I got them free. I reached out in the darkness and touched what seemed to be a tractor wheel.

Wha-wha-what was going on?

POLICE CONSTABLE GAVIN OWEN

Yes, we did receive a call that night and it was from Mr Burrowes. We know Mr Burrowes down at the station. In the past he has called us about the government spying on him through his TV set. On another occasion he thought a helicopter flying over the mountains was the government taking photographs of him. He is an eccentric gentleman, shall we say?

We told him we would call by the next day to see that he was all right. That's what a lot of policing is these days

– reassuring vulnerable members of the community that everything is going to be all right.

THE SMILER

I felt around the walls. There was no way out. I pushed against the door. It wouldn't give. I groped my way along the tractor to the ignition. The key was in it.

GODFATHER GIDEON

I heard the Massey's engine start up.

Lock the workshop, I thought. I was sprinting across the courtyard when the tractor smashed through the door of its shed like a fist through a paper bag.

I hid behind the shed.

The man sat in the tractor seat, gazing at where his car had been.

'Where's my car?' he yelled. 'Where's my motor?'

He jumped down from the tractor, ran into the house. I heard the smashing of dishes as he looked for me. He came out and opened the door to the taxi. The key was in my pocket.

He looked around wildly. 'I'll be back,' he yelled. 'I promise you that!'

Then he jumped back on to the tractor, crashed the gears into place and set off down the hill.

A broken chair, smashed crockery and now a stolen tractor. It was a bad, bad evening.

Mark could drive. I have to admit it. It was as if he had been on the roads for years.

We decided to follow the signs to Newport, the nearest big town, and then head towards London. All that mattered was distance between us and Prendergast.

It was getting dark.

At some point I asked if we were all sure that we had cleared the rooms at Hill Farm of our possessions.

It was then that Trix said, 'I couldn't find my T-shirt. Did anyone see it?'

We drove east. Mark took it slow, but not so slow as to be suspicious. Every five minutes or so, Jade rang her brother Brad to tell him where we had reached.

'Maybe you should give the guy a rest from calls,' Mark said at one stage.

'Got to keep ringing,' said Jade. 'Else Brad will forget where he's meant to be driving. His short-term memory is totally shot.'

'Oh great,' murmured Mark.

Sitting behind in the back seat, Trix and I exchanged glances.

We had been driving for about an hour when Mark noticed that the diesel tank was only a quarter full. Pulling into a service station was too risky so we agreed to drive to an isolated spot and meet Brad there.

'Oh.' Jade tapped her forehead. 'That's what I keep meaning to say. We've got to disguise Trix before we meet Brad.'

'*What?*' I leaned forward. 'Can't we trust him? I thought he was your brother.'

'There are brothers and brothers,' said Jade. 'All I'm saying is that we have to treat Brad carefully. I'll tell him in my own time and my own way. He shouldn't know Trix is Little Trixie until I've explained the situation very slowly and carefully.'

'How can we disguise Trix?' said Mark. 'We've only got our own clothes.'

'Pull in when you can, Mark.' Trix spoke quietly. 'I'm going to need a T-shirt and some trousers from Wiki, your baseball cap, Mark, and, Jade, I'll need your dark glasses.'

'No way,' said Jade. 'Those are Ray-Bans. You don't use Ray-Bans as a disguise. You just don't.'

'You're going to dress up as a boy?' I asked Trix.

'We all have to make sacrifices,' said Trix.

JADE

Mark pulled off the road into this gate entrance. Wiki got into the front of the car. I sat with Trix and the boys' bags.

As Mark drove, Trix disguised herself. Baseball cap, extremely expensive and stylish shades, baggy T-shirt and trousers.

She looked ridiculous, pathetic, totally absurd.

She looked like a boy.

BRAD HART

OK, so you want to know about my little sister. She's the white sheep in the family. My older brother George and I

169

live life on the edge. Parents? Careers? The law? We just don't care.

We live by one simple, beautiful, golden rule: LIFE IS SHORT – HAVE FUN.

JADE

We were getting low on gas. Mark took the SUV off the main road. We wound through some country roads until we reached a village of about five houses and a village green. We parked up in a dark spot and waited.

I rang Brad. 'We're in a place called Kington,' I said.

'Great. Lemme check on the navigator. Is that Kington in Scotland, Cornwall or Wiltshire?'

'Brad, I'm pretty sure it's not in Scotland or Cornwall.'

'You're pretty sure? D'you actually know you're not in Scotland?'

'It was a *joke*, Brad. Kington, Wiltshire, is where we are. Near some swings and a little green. Look for a big black SUV.'

'What? It says five hundred and eighty miles on the navigator.'

I closed my eyes and took a deep breath. 'I said, *not* Cornwall, Brad. Wiltshire.'

'Oh, right. I'll be there in about thirty minutes.'

MARK

We were in a stranger's car, parked in some little village

deep in the countryside. We were waiting for someone we had never met to take us we didn't know where. I'd left the engine running, so at least it was warm in the car.

Then the engine began missing.

'There goes our diesel,' I said. The engine died.

WIKI

We sat in the dark, each of us thinking our own, mostly depressing, thoughts.

After about half an hour, Jade rang her brother. Here's how the conversation went:

'Where are you, bro? . . . Almost there, that's great . . . No, it's not on the outskirts of a town . . . Supermarket? What supermarket? Are you sure – ? . . . *Kington*, not Kingston, Jesus, Brad. Kington in Wiltshire . . . So how many miles are you away now? . . . Eighty-six miles. Oh great, that's just terrific, Brad . . . Repeat after me: Kington, Wiltshire.'

She snapped the phone shut. 'Brad took a wrong turning,' she said. Staring out of the window, she held out a hand in Trix's direction. 'Gimme my Ray-Bans.' Trix passed them to her.

We sat in silence for a few more seconds.

'What?' she said suddenly. 'What's with the heavy silence? Anyone can take a wrong turn.'

Trix put a hand on her shoulder.

JADE

Don't you just hate it when people start feeling sorry for you? Life's bumming out in some way but you're keeping it together somehow. Then someone puts a hand on your shoulder and someone else asks if you're OK and, whammo, you're gone.

MARK

'Are you all right, Jade?' This was Wiki.

Result? Niagara Falls.

For about a minute, Jade stared out of the window and sobbed away like someone had died. Then she wiped her nose, sniffed hard, and took a deep breath.

'I guess I'd better tell you about my family,' she said.

JADE

We all have our secrets, but mine's bigger than most.

Fact is, Brad and George, my dysfunctional brothers, are pretty much all the family I have.

My father's this mega-rich businessman who owns a chain of casinos in Las Vegas. My mom's English. Way back when she was working as a dancer in Vegas she met Mr Rick Hart. They got it together, got married, got three kids, got bored, got divorced.

Mom came back to England when I was about ten. She met this record-producer guy called Ziggy Rasmussen. They got it together, got married, etc., etc., but it turns out

172

that Ziggy's not too crazy about the whole family thing. He tells Mom it's us or him. I get shipped off to boarding school. My brothers move into an apartment in London.

Because here's the deal. Back in Vegas, my father's got another family. He has 'moved on', he says. He gives us each this big trust fund to pay for our education. When we hit eighteen, each of us gets seriously rich. The only condition is that he doesn't want to see us or hear from us again.

Mom and Ziggy liked to travel. Most of their travelling seemed to take place during the school vacations. Pretty soon I started staying with my two brothers. A couple of years ago, the marriage went south, but Mom's kinda got into the habit of travelling. The last I heard, she'd met this barman in Barbados.

A few weeks before, she told Brad that we'd be having a family Christmas. We're not holding our breath.

WIKI

Jade told us her story in a flat, cold voice.

When she finished, she turned to us and said, 'You tell anyone about this and you die, right?'

We muttered our agreement.

'I only told you because you're about to meet my brothers. The only other person I've told is Holly.'

'How old are your brothers?' Mark asked.

'Twenty-four and twenty-two.'

'What do they do?'

Jade gave a little laugh. 'What would you do if you had a big fat trust fund? They spend it.'

MAJOR GRAHAM BARTON

Kington residents have complained in the past about teenagers hanging around the green, causing trouble.

What has been done by the authorities? Absolutely sugar all!

I told my wife June that I'd be getting evidence to show the police the kind of problems Kington has with youths, yobs, boy racers and the like. That night I had noticed the big car by the green. There were several people inside – teenagers, I suspected. They were there, waiting, for almost two hours.

It worried me, frankly. I told June that I would be staying up to keep an eye on the situation. One can never be too careful these days.

WIKI

Soon after midnight, we heard a high, angry buzz in the distance. It sounded very like a sports car being driven at high speed.

'I'm hoping that's not Brad,' said Trix.

'Hope on,' said Jade. 'Get your Ray-Bans on, Mr Trix.'

Moments later, a silver Porsche turned the corner and braked. Then, seeing us, it accelerated with a roar of the engine and stopped with a squeal of tyres in front of us.

JADE

Picture it. A tiny, cute-as-pie English village at dead of night, and suddenly there's my big brother Brad burning rubber and revving the engine of his Porsche.

Just what we needed, right?

He got out of the car with a, 'Yo, sis, how ya goin'?'

'Hello, Brad.' I managed a smile. 'These are my friends Mark, Wiki and –' I suddenly realized we hadn't fixed up Trix with a boy's name. I grabbed one from the murky depths of my brain – 'Tim.'

'Tim?' Trix turned away in disgust at my choice of name. OK, so it wasn't great but it was the best I could come up with.

'Hanging out with the guys, eh, sis?' said Brad. 'I'm not going to ask what you've been up to.'

'That's good, Brad.' I gave my words maximum sarcasm. 'Because I wouldn't tell you anyway.'

'Great 911 Carrera.' Mark wandered around Brad's car. 'But maybe a tad small for five people, don't you think?'

'Nah,' Brad jumped into the driver's seat. 'I've had seven in here. After a party – it was wild, man. You two guys get in the back and my sis and Tim will keep me company in the front with the bags.'

Mark got in. Wiki squeezed in beside him. Trix – or rather, Tim – sat on my lap.

'Hope you guys are good friends,' said Brad, putting the car into gear and driving off so fast that each of us nearly left our heads behind.

'There's only one way to drive with my brother,' I shouted from the front of the car. 'With your eyes tight shut and praying every inch of the way.'

MAJOR GRAHAM BARTON

When a silver sports car turned up making the most infernal racket, I reached for my camera.

Three boys and a girl got out of the big vehicle. A long-haired youth emerged from the sports car. They didn't stay long, I'll admit, but I sensed they were trouble.

That's how we are in Kington. We take action. I got one perfect photograph when the five hooligans were standing in the headlights of the sports car.

If there was trouble, I had the evidence.

WIKI

It was a journey from hell. Jade's brother burned up the motorway towards London, heavy metal blaring from the sound system.

It was the early hours of the morning when we arrived in London. Somewhere in the centre of the city, we pulled up outside a large, modern building. Our bodies aching, our ears ringing from the noise, we walked through a brightly lit lobby and took the lift to the fourteenth floor.

Brad opened the door to his flat. It consisted of a big room which looked as if a bomb had hit it – beer cans, CDs and ashtrays were all over the floor.

'You guys coming out clubbing?' Brad asked.

'We're bushed,' said Jade.

'There are mattresses round the place. You kids make yourself at home,' said Brad.

Then he was gone.

There were mattresses all right, but finding them in the ruin of the flat wasn't easy. In the end I crashed out in my clothes beside Mark on a big evil-smelling mattress that was under a small mountain of unwashed clothes in the sitting room. Trix and Jade found another mattress on the floor of one of the bedrooms and slept there.

HOLLY

When I awoke on day two in the so-called civilized world, things became distinctly weird. The publicity agent with the big hair, Vogel, had arranged for what he called a 'photo opportunity' that morning. My mother was to take me round to Trix's house, where I'd be snapped having morning tea with her mother and stepfather. The idea was to show how Trix's family and friends were there for each other at this difficult time ('Barf,' as Jade would say).

We got to the house soon after ten. The photographer was already there. Eva, my mother, Jason the stepfather, Eddison Vogel and little me sat in a conservatory. A maid served us tea. We prepared to look tragic for the camera.

Then the phone rang.

The maid went to answer it. She came back. It was Detective Inspector Cartwright, she said. He insisted on speaking to Eva.

When she returned, she was in a state of shock. She sat down slowly on her chair and whispered, 'They've found Trixie's T-shirt.'

DETECTIVE INSPECTOR BARRY CARTWRIGHT

You're not supposed to be emotional in this game but, just for a moment in my office, I lost it. I may be a policeman but I'm a human being too. By now it was almost as if Little Trixie was part of my family.

The call came from the office of the Show Us You Care fund. They had received a parcel. In it was a T-shirt Little Trixie used to wear. It had been slashed with a knife.

No message. Nothing. But there didn't have to be.

Tears pricked my eyes. Sometimes this is a dirty, dirty job.

WIKI

We awoke late the following morning. By daylight the flat looked even worse than it had the previous night.

I walked into the kitchen. Jade was standing in front of a sink in which dirty dishes and glasses from the last month or so were piled high.

'Beyond the valley of the gross,' she said in a faint voice.

JADE

I admit it. My brothers have never been that hot on housekeeping. I'll go further. My brothers have never been that hot on anything. Except partying. They are very, very good at that.

'Where's Brad?' Wiki asked.

I glanced at my watch. It was almost eleven in the morning. 'He'll be out for a while yet,' I said. 'George and Brad usually go to bed at about lunchtime.'

Mark appeared at the door. For the first time in living history, he was lost for words.

'Maybe we should tidy up,' said Trix.

'Are you kidding?' I laughed. 'I've spent my life clearing up after my brothers. That is so over.'

I went to the fridge, opened it.

'Looks like we've got a choice for breakfast,' I said. 'Beer, beer or more beer.'

I sniffed some milk. Heave. 'Maybe someone had better do some shopping,' I said.

'I'll go,' said Mark.

'Yeah, I'll come too.' Wiki seemed unusually eager. 'I need a breath of fresh air.'

MARK

When we got downstairs, we discovered that we were in one of those parts in the centre of the city where there are bars and hotels and expensive clothes shops but nowhere to buy bread and butter.

Wiki saw a street sign. 'We're in Mayfair,' he said.

'The middle of London,' I said. 'A great place for a hideout, I must say.'

We walked, taking care to remember which way we came. It took us over half an hour to find some bread, butter, milk and orange juice.

We were back at the flat soon after midday. One glance at the girls' faces told us that something had happened while we were away.

HOLLY

As soon as I got home, I went to my room and dialled Jade's number. The whole T-shirt thing had thrown me. It had to be them who had sent it. What were they thinking of? It had been my big fear that without me there to keep things more or less sensible, the gang would do something wild. But this was beyond wild. It was crazy.

Jade picked up on the second ring.

'Have you gone mad?' I asked. 'Sending Trix's T-shirt

through the post. What's going on out there?'

'Holly, calm down.' Suddenly Jade sounded weirdly normal, almost grown up. I could hardly recognize her for a moment. 'First, we are not "out there". We're in London. And we've sent nothing to anyone.'

So, we unscrambled. Jade told me about the scary visitor in Wales – how they had left Gideon, the whole strange business about staying with her brothers George and Brad.

'Your brothers? You've always said they were a couple of –' I swallowed back the swear word that was on the tip of my tongue. 'You said that they were not always entirely reliable.'

Jade seemed to take a deep breath. 'We didn't exactly have a choice, Holly,' she said through gritted teeth. 'Tell me about this T-shirt.'

I told her. We agreed to talk later. I had only one thought in my mind. The game was up. We had done our best, but our plan was spinning out of control.

Surely even Trix Johansson-Bell, the most stubborn girl in the world, would see that.

JADE

When I told her about the T-shirt, Trix gave a little gasp. 'My mum,' she said. 'My poor mum. She'll be panicking. I must do something.'

'Wait,' I said. 'Let's be sensible about this.'

Trix looked at me, surprised. Tell the truth, I was kind of startled myself. I have never knowingly spoken the words "Let's be sensible about this" in my entire life.

Then I did something else that was weird. I put my arm around Trix. I felt her lean away from me, then relax.

'Let's just wait till my brothers get back,' I said. 'We're in this together, right?'

Trix gave an angry little laugh. 'Oh yeah, they'll *definitely* come up with a great idea.'

EVA JOHANSSON

Before that terrible day, I had held myself together in a proud way – I was strong as a mother should be.

Eddison had told me that, by showing what he said was 'tragic dignity', I was reminding the world that even celebrities can be brave. 'Eva, honey,' he said, 'you've become a role model – a role model for the nation. Maybe even an international role model.'

An international role model? Me? I could hardly believe it. The awful grey cloud of Trixie's disappearance had a silver lining.

'Eve, babe,' said Eddison, 'this is highly confidential. But there's talk of your being given a special nomination at the Share Awards on Sunday night.'

'The Share Awards?' I could hardly believe my ears.

Eddison nodded, smiling. 'Live on terrestrial TV. Syndicated throughout the world. Highlights repeated throughout the week.'

For a celebrity like me, the Share Awards are the ultimate. They are the annual occasion when world-class models, actors and TV personalities gather to celebrate what is important in life – love, bravery, the family, kids. They mix with ordinary people and give prizes to the Teacher of the

Year, the Foster Parent of the Year, the Differently Abled Child of the Year and so on.

'To recognize your bravery.' There was a smile on Eddison's face. 'At the moment, they're calling it the Share Celebrity Mother of the Year.'

I was moved – of course I was. Who wouldn't want to be voted the Share Celebrity Mother of the Year, live on TV before an international audience?

'But, Eddison, the T-shirt,' I said. 'That will change everything. People don't like to be frightened or depressed at the Share Awards. They're all about feeling good, about hope.'

Eddison, in his quiet, calm voice, put me right again.

'Wrong,' he said. 'The T-shirt clinches it. When the news breaks, there's no way that the Share Awards will drop their plans for the Celebrity Mother of the Year award. Babe, you're a shoo-in.'

WIKI

'Something's happened,' Jade said as we let ourselves back into the flat. I swear I was beginning to dread those words. It seemed that whenever Mark and I turned our backs, something would happen.

They told us about the T-shirt.

'It must have been the psycho,' said Mark.

'Why would he want to steal Trix's T-shirt?' I asked.

'Yeah,' Jade muttered. 'What kind of fashion victim would want that?'

Trix ignored her. 'We've got to tell my parents not to worry,' she said. 'I'll send Mum a text tonight.'

'They'll trace it,' said Mark.

'We've got to do something,' I said. 'Somehow we've got to get word to Trix's mum.'

MARK

We were still discussing how to send a text without revealing where we were when there was the sound of a key fumbling at the lock of the flat. It was almost two o'clock in the afternoon. The Hart brothers were back from their night out.

'Trix!' said Wiki. 'Get your dark glasses on. You're Tim, remember.'

Muttering rebelliously, Trix walked off.

Seconds later, the front door opened and two guys, one of whom was Brad, staggered in.

'Hi, boys.' Jade spoke casually, then turned to Wik and me. 'These are my brothers,' she said. 'Brad, you know. George, you don't.'

The two guys stood there, swaying slightly, looking confused. They were what my dad calls 'feeling no pain'.

'Brats,' George drawled. 'In the apartment. What's going on?'

'I told you, man,' said Brad. 'That was where I went last night. I had to drive around half of England to pick up Jade and her boyfriends. They'll be hanging out with us for a few days.'

'Yeah, yeah, whatevs.' George sounded unimpressed by the idea.

I looked at Jade, expecting one of her snappy comebacks. She sipped her juice, saying nothing.

'Where's Tim?' asked Brad.

'Here.' Trix appeared in the doorway of the bedroom, her Ray-Bans in place.

'Hey, guy.' Brad gave her a broad, drunken grin. 'How's it hangin'?'

Trix hesitated for a moment. 'Pretty well, thank you,' she said coldly.

'I'm wrecked.' George lurched towards one of the bedrooms. 'Laters, guys.'

WIKI

We stood there, feeling slightly embarrassed.

'Welcome to the Hart family home,' said Jade.

She seemed to be about to say something when Brad reappeared, now without his trousers.

'Hey, sis,' he said to Jade. 'How about cooking us up something special tonight, huh? Just like the old days.'

He looked at me. 'She's an ace cook, man. I love it when she comes to stay.'

'There's nothing in the fridge.' Jade spoke quietly. I sensed that she wasn't thrilled by the way her brothers treated her like an unpaid servant.

'Just tell her what you like to eat, guys,' said George. 'Jade cooks most anything.'

I noticed that Trix was looking pale, a sure sign that she was about to blow her top.

'I've heard that guys can cook too,' she said, smiling dangerously.

'That's interesting, *Tim*,' I said, thinking quickly. 'What do you cook?'

She blinked quickly, remembering just in time that she was meant to be a boy.

'Risotto,' she said. 'Tell you what – that's what we'll have tonight.'

'A dude cooking risotto.' Brad shook his head as he headed back to the bedroom. 'I've heard everything now.'

PETE BELL

In another lifetime, when I was a successful reporter, I used to be asked the secret of successful investigations.

The answer was simple. You ask questions. You work round the clock. You keep pushing against the door. Eventually someone will say something that gives you a clue. You ask more questions. You push harder. There's a chink of light. Eventually, if you're lucky, the door begins to open.

That day, that dark day, when the slashed T-shirt turned up, I began to see things more clearly.

The cop Cartwright was useless. My ex-wife and her creep of a publicist Eddison Vogel were playing some kind of weird game of their own. In the fog of egos, the one person who mattered in all this, Trix, was getting lost.

I hit the phones. I called all the journalists I knew who were covering the case. I asked questions.

They were, of course, pleased to hear from old Pete Bell. Maybe I could give them an interview. They had written about the mother of Little Trixie. Talking to the daddy would give them a new angle.

One after the other, I told them that I was talking to nobody. Right now, I wasn't interested in helping them. They needed to help me.

And suddenly all my old pals were not quite so friendly. The case was hotting up. They were under pressure from their editors. They knew stuff, sure, but right now they were only rumours. It would be wrong to pass them on to me.

'You know how it is, Pete,' one of them said. 'You've been there yourself. You want to be the person to break the story.'

'You see,' I said, 'to me it's not a story. It's my daughter. It's a matter of life and death.'

'Give me an exclusive interview and we can talk, Pete.'

I hung up. There was one golden rule I had forgotten. Journalists don't help journalists.

Late that night, I took out my old contacts book and leafed through its pages. As if I were being guided in some way, I found myself staring at a name I had all but forgotten.

Detective Inspector Trevor Jones. Retired. Also known as 'the Grey Fox'.

Jones knew more about crime than most policemen had forgotten. He had caught criminals. He had become friends with criminals. Then he had become a criminal.

There was only one problem. He hated my guts.

EX-DETECTIVE INSPECTOR TREVOR JONES

No comment.

EVA JOHANSSON

The police had a plan. That was what Barry Cartwright told me and I had no alternative but to believe him. They wanted twenty-four hours while the discovery of Trixie's T-shirt remained secret. The next day, the news would be released and I would appear at a press conference.

It was a strange day, waiting for the next move. Eddison was with other clients. Jason was working. Even the Drunk seemed to be off on some mad project of his own.

Eva Johansson was feeling very, very alone.

PETE BELL

There was no point in telephoning the Grey Fox. Ever since he had been released from prison, he had refused all requests for interviews. He was that very unusual thing – a famous person who is not a blabbermouth.

When I was working, Jones had been one of the most senior policemen in the land – a quiet, grey-haired man who had a reputation for catching the bad guys.

Until one day someone investigated rumours that he was taking holidays in Spain with bank robbers. Someone started investigating the investigator. The Grey Fox found himself hunted. Someone discovered that he had been taking bribes from the very people he was meant to be bringing to justice. There was a scandal, a court case. He was given a five-year jail sentence for corruption and perjury.

The name of that someone who ended the career of Detective Inspector Trevor Jones? You've guessed it, of course.

EX-DETECTIVE INSPECTOR TREVOR JONES

I will tell you this and nothing else. If there was anyone in the world I would happily never have seen again, it was Pete Bell.

I live a quiet life. I'm retired. I've made mistakes in the past. We all have. I've moved on.

But then there he was, the piece of scum who destroyed my life. Older, uglier, sadder, but there was no mistaking him. He stood there on my doorstep.

And would you believe it? Pete Bell was actually asking me a favour.

PETE BELL

The Grey Fox was an old man but, when I rang the front doorbell of his little semi-detached house in South London, he recognized me at once.

When I said I was looking for a favour, the expression on his face remained as blank as it always was.

'No way,' he growled.

'Trevor,' I said. 'It's about my daughter. She's disappeared.'

'I read about it. Very sad.'

He tried to close the door on me. I put a foot forward and held it fast. It was quite like old times.

'I don't want to talk about the past,' I said. 'Listen. I'm desperate.'

The old man looked at me sullenly.

'I heard you are a drunk these days.'

'We've both had tough times,' I said.

'You're not writing about this, are you?'

'I just want to find my daughter.'

He stepped back. 'Five minutes,' he muttered.

I stepped into the dark hall. There was still a smell of breakfast in the air, and I heard the sound of someone in the kitchen.

'I'll be in the front room,' he called out.

We went into a small room and sat in small identical armchairs on each side of a sad little gas fire.

'You've read about the case, have you?' I asked.

The Grey Fox shook his head. 'I gave up newspapers years ago. I know the kind of scum who write for them.'

I let the insult pass.

'I've seen stuff on the TV news,' he muttered.

'The person that's holding her has just sent us her T-shirt. It seems to have been stabbed.'

The old man raised his eyes. Nothing can surprise or shock an ex-copper.

I pressed on. 'Who would do that sort of thing?' I asked.

'An idiot,' he said. 'Someone who's not thinking straight. He's handing over evidence voluntarily.'

'Why would he do that?'

He shrugged, but behind his hooded eyes I sensed that the cunning old brain was cranking into action.

'Your wife got enemies, has she?' he asked casually.

'Ex-wife. She left me,' I said.

'Not surprised,' he said. 'She was always well out of your class.'

I waited. It paid to be patient with the Grey Fox.

'He wants to hurt her. He wants to get to her. That's what this is about. Some sort of revenge.'

'But—'

'Listen, Bell.' He stared at me and I was aware at that moment that his loathing for me was as powerful as it ever was. 'I love kiddies like anyone but, to be honest, it doesn't break my heart to see you in pain.'

I looked away.

'At least you know how it feels now.' He stood up. 'Now get out and leave me alone. I would say I'm sorry I couldn't help you but then I'd be lying.'

I followed him out of the room.

He opened the front door.

I gave it one last try. 'If anything occurs to you –' I reached into my back pocket for a tattered old card with my address and telephone number on – 'could you just call me?'

He looked at the card and laughed nastily. 'I wouldn't dream of it,' he said, turning back into the house. 'Now get out and leave me alone.'

I put the card back in my pocket and left without another word.

JADE

My brothers: in a way, they were the perfect hosts. They were so wrapped up in their own little world that they hardly saw us.

That evening, while we were busying around the kitchen and Trix was cooking her famous risotto, the phone rang. George took it in his bedroom. After a mumbled conversation, he stumbled out in a T-shirt and jockey shorts and thumped on Brad's door.

'Party over at Heidi's,' he said, then fell into the bathroom.

Fifteen minutes later, it was, 'Catch ya later, sis,' as they headed out the door for the night.

'What?' Trix stood in front of a saucepan, a wooden spoon in her hand. 'What about my risotto?'

'That's my brothers for you,' I said.

WIKI

Over supper we talked about how to get word to Trix's mother that, in spite of the slashed T-shirt, her daughter had not fallen into the hands of a mad knifeman.

'We've got to text her,' said Trix. 'Sometimes she doesn't look at her computer for days. She's never far from her phone.'

'They'll trace it,' I said. 'They'll know whose mobile it is and where they are. We'd be as good as handing ourselves in.'

'Maybe I should just call her,' said Trix. 'I could speak really quickly, then hang up.'

I shook my head. It was the same problem.

'We're kind of screwed,' said Jade.

I noticed a laptop lying amid some empty beer cans in the corner.

'Maybe not,' I said.

JADE

Frankly, the moment when Professor Nerdy Two-Brain Wiki Church started playing with the laptop, occasionally muttering to himself in some geeky code of his own, the rest of us began to zone out.

He had told us that there might be a way to get a text message to Trix's mom from Brad's computer without anyone being able to know where it came from. There were websites which provided anonymous texts but, according to the professor, they could still be traced back. He muttered about protocols and embedded thingies and interrupted control systems. There was quite a lot of bouncing off this and that. An illegal server in Korea came into it somewhere.

Give us a break, Wik. Just do it and spare us the explanations. After a while, we left him to it and watched a bit of TV.

After about half an hour, he called out, 'OK, give me the message you want to send. It'll go through at eleven a.m. Korean time.'

'I don't want to rain on your parade, Wik,' I said, 'but I have bad news. We are not actually in Korea.'

'Sorry,' he said, tapping happily at his keyboard like a concert pianist. 'That'll be two a.m. our time. It's completely untraceable.'

Big admission now: I was almost impressed.

WIKI

Our problem was: how to convince Eva Johansson that she

really was hearing from her daughter. For all she knew, it could be the Mad Knifeman trying to trick her. Or maybe even one of those sick practical jokes that some people like to play.

I had the computer primed for (illegal) action. As the other three stood behind me, staring at the blank message screen, it became clear that our problems were not over.

It was Jade who came up with the solution.

'Here we go,' she said. 'You include something in the text that no one else in the world except you and your mom are supposed to know.'

Trix closed her eyes for a moment. Then slowly, incredibly, she began to smile.

JADE

It was a short message, but a good one.

'Mum Im OK. Ignre T-shirt. Be hme soon. Love you. Trix xxx. So you no its rlly me – Im telling u smthing only u & I no. Lst yr u hd csmtc surgery on yr bum!'

V Day + 17

EVA JOHANSSON

Not my bottom! Anything but that. Please, Trix. No.

It was the early hours of the morning when the cellphone beside my bed made the little chirruping noise that means a text has arrived.

Who would be contacting me at that hour? It occurred to me that my agent Lori may have been texting from the coast with news about my major film project.

To avoid waking Jason, I crept out to the bathroom, shut the door and turned on the light. I read the text.

At first the words of the little screen made my heart leap. Trix was all right! My little Trixie was safe! Everything was going to be fine.

But there was something wrong, something fishy about this. I sat on the edge of the bath and read the text again. Slowly, my joy – the simple joy of a mother – began to ebb away. I felt sick.

There was no doubt about it. I was being blackmailed – blackmailed about something very intimate and secret to a woman. At the very moment my career as an actress was taking off again, a horrible, horrible story about my derrière would get into the papers. It would finish me. Not so long ago, I had been on the shortlist for the famous Rear of the Year Award. At that time, I told reporters that I had never had any surgery. If the truth about my bottom came out, I could kiss goodbye to any chance of being Share Celebrity Mother of the Year.

But at least no one else had read it. That was a good thing. I deleted it, then tried to go back to sleep.

Two restless hours later, I drifted off. When I awoke, Jason had already left for work.

My heart thumping, I picked up the cellphone and checked for messages. There was nothing.

Perhaps I had dreamed it. Yes, that was it. It must have been a terrible dream, caused by the stress of my situation.

And you don't tell people about dreams, do you?

EDDISON VOGEL

In the news-management game, balance is important. The police were going to announce that the kidnapper had sent the T-shirt of Little Trixie to the Show Us You Care fund. I had told Barry Cartwright that he should suggest this was a breakthrough in the case.

'Is it?' he asked me, fiddling nervously with his dark glasses.

'Yes, it is, Barry. Forensics, the way it was packed, handwriting, blah-blah-blah. Come on, you're a policeman. You know how to make things up.'

'That's not funny,' Barry muttered. Then he added, 'But leave it with me.'

So the public would think that the net was closing. But still we needed to get people involved. That night, the news bulletins would lead with the story that the family of Tragic Trixie (I started using the word 'tragic' in my interviews; the journalists picked it up like well-trained pooches hearing a dog-whistle) were hiring a specialist detective agency and an international scientific team to help in the search.

The Show Us You Care fund was in more desperate need of funds than ever.

Finally, there was Eva, my star player. That afternoon she would make a heartbreaking public appeal. People love a heartbreaking public appeal. After that, her spot on the Share Awards would be assured.

Mix the positive with the negative. Keep the news moving. That's the way to play it.

THE SMILER

Me, I won't have a word said against the police. They have a tough job and they try their very best.

Sometimes they're even quite efficient. A mere two days after it had been stolen, they rang to tell me that my car had been found in a place called Kington.

'Oh, thank goodness, officer,' I said in my most polite telephone voice. 'I've been worried sick about it. It was stolen on Tuesday.'

The copper asked me a few questions about how it had disappeared. I had called in at the village shop, I told him, had left the keys in the ignition ('I'm a very trusting person, officer') and when I came out it was gone.

I put down the phone. Ten minutes later, my neighbour David, a silly old man who's so scared of me I can ask him to do anything, was driving me towards Swindon police station.

When I walked in, I was prepared for trouble.

There are very few police computers on which the name Charles Prendergast doesn't light up in red and send off alarm signals, but they looked at my vehicle-registration documents, took a statement and gave me the keys.

'Have you any idea who might have done this terrible thing, officer?' I asked the uniformed cop at the desk.

'To tell the truth, Mr Prendergast, we're so busy these days that car theft is low on our list of priorities. We have to concentrate our efforts on serious crime.'

'I understand, officer,' I said, picking up the keys.

Serious crime, eh? The boys in blue were about to discover just how serious crime could get.

PETE

I spent the morning online, reading press articles about the life and times of my ex-wife Eva Johansson.

Who would hate a semi-famous actress with an ego the size of the Empire State Building? Quite a lot of people, it turned out, but none of them would be crazy enough to kidnap her daughter for revenge.

I thought back to my conversation with the Grey Fox. What were his words when I had said goodbye to him? 'At least you know how it feels now.'

'Of course.' I whispered the words. What a fool I had been.

It wasn't Eva the kidnapper was trying to hurt. It was me.

JADE

We awoke mid-morning and had breakfast in silence. The text had been sent. Now it was just a question of waiting until Trix, our mighty leader, decided on the next move.

More because there was nothing else to do than anything else, we began to put my brothers' flat in order.

The last thing we needed was to be thrown out on to the street by the Brothers Grim.

THE SMILER

I drove the Discovery back to the village where it had been found. It was time for the Smiler to turn detective.

The village of Kington was one of those dozy little two-horse towns where people come to die.

I knocked on a door. An old lady opened it. Something about my face seemed to scare her.

'I'm terribly sorry to bother you,' I said, 'but my car was stolen two days ago and left here.'

'No.' The old bird looked as if she were about to faint clean away. 'I don't see anything ever. I believe in minding my own business. So sorry.'

She closed the door in my face, the silly old trout.

There was no answer at the cottage next door. I crossed a lane and rang the bell of a little cottage with loads of roses around the front door.

An officer-type – moustache, half-moon glasses, the works – opened the door.

'Can I help you?' he said.

It turned out that he could.

MAJOR GRAHAM BARTON

It is very rare in life that one's efforts to fight crime are rewarded, but this was one of them.

The chap at my door, a rather rough-looking type, turned out to be the victim of the youths I had seen on the green.

'So my instinct was right,' I said, having invited him into the snug. 'I sensed that those youths were up to no good.'

'You were very, very right, sir,' said the gentleman, whose name he had said was Mr Smiley. 'Do you happen to remember what they looked like?'

I chuckled. 'I can do better than that.' I walked to my desk and picked up a print of the photograph I had snapped of the yobs on the green. I handed it to Mr Smiley.

'Oh yes,' he said, holding it in his hand. 'You did excellent work, Mr Barton. I expect you handed this to the police, did you?'

'Actually, no,' I said. 'I was rather assuming they might contact me.'

'Tell you what,' said Mr Smiley, 'I'm working closely with the car-crime unit in this case. Would it be all right if I handed this evidence to them myself?'

Of course, I agreed, putting my name and telephone number on the back of the print.

THE SMILER

Four kids. One bloke. My Discovery. And a Porsche. The number plate was as clear as daylight:

I have friends everywhere. It was time to call my contact in the vehicle-registration office.

The Smiler was back in business.

PETE BELL

Like the Grey Fox, I don't like dwelling on the past, but now I had research to do. Who hated me enough to want to harm my daughter? I climbed a ladder in the attic, where in three large boxes I kept the newspaper cuttings from the days when I was a crime reporter. I heaved them down the ladder and started reading.

The articles, once so proudly cut out, were now dusty and yellowing. They reminded me uncomfortably of a time when I still mattered.

After two hours I had the names of three people who could say that, if it hadn't been for one nosy journalist, they would still be free.

There was Trevor Jones, the Grey Fox. I knew he was in the clear. A nasty piece of work called Colin Parker was capable of almost anything, but he was still serving time for murder, manslaughter, grievous bodily harm and a few lesser crimes of violence. Finally there was Charles Prendergast, better known as 'The Smiler'.

I switched on the computer and did some Googling. It took no more than five minutes to find the latest cutting of a small item from a local newspaper in South London.

BANK ROBBER RELEASED

Charles Prendergast, who became notorious during the mid-1990s for a series of violent robberies, was released from prison this week, having served an eight-year sentence. Prendergast, who was nicknamed 'The Smiler' as a result of a scar to the face, told reporters that he planned to start a new life in Wales.

It was a far cry from the glory days when the Smiler's ugly face was on the front pages of every newspaper, but it told me what I wanted to know.

All that the police told me about the slashed T-shirt was that it had been sent from Wales. I picked up my telephone and dialled Barry Cartwright. He was busy talking to the press as usual.

EVA JOHANSSON

It was a tough call, that press conference, when I had to sit beside Barry Cartwright as he talked about the T-shirt to the world's press. I managed to hold back the tears until the very last sentence of my statement. There was a moment when the detective realized that here was a mother in agony. He put his arm around my shoulders in a strange and comforting way. It was the photograph that would appear on most of the front pages the next day.

EDDISON VOGEL

Little Trixie was suddenly Tragic Trixie. The press went

crazy. Money poured in from the public – the Show Us You Care fund had hit the million mark by lunchtime. During a House of Commons debate that afternoon, the Prime Minister referred to 'the young idealist Trixie Johansson-Bell, who is in our minds today and who is at the mercy of a profound evil'.

Tragic Trixie. Innocence betrayed. The young idealist pitted against profound evil. Her fate involved all of us. She represented all that was good: generosity, courage, childhood. Her fate made every adult feel guilty, involved.

The news bulletins over the next twenty-four hours would ignore everything else.

GEORGE HART

There's a downtime. It's between when I wake, usually about six o'clock in the evening, and when my bro and I go out clubbing, which is usually around eleven.

I fix breakfast – toast and beer – maybe take in a film on the movie channel. Sometimes I play online poker. It can be a bummer, that downtime. Five long hours of sitting around waiting for the action to begin.

But that particular evening was just fine. I awoke and wandered, still half-asleep in my jockey shorts, into the kitchen. It was kind of tidy. It smelt different – almost, I dunno, clean. There were voices in the lounge. The kids were there. They were doing the whole housework thing. One was tidying the CDs, another collecting up clothes. The little guy in shades – Tim – was actually wiping down the insides of the window, which had become kind of nicotined up since we had been there.

'Hey, hey, hey.' I walked over to Tim and took the cloth from him. 'House rule, man. No guy carries a duster in this apartment. We get chick cleaners in to do a clean-up. Or my little sister.'

And Tim took the cloth back from me, cool as you like.

'I like it,' he said in this strange, strangled voice.

Weird guy.

MARK

When Trix is angry, she doesn't go red like most people. She goes deathly white, as if her rage has made her physically ill.

That's how she went then, grabbing the cloth from Jade's older brother and turning to go back to work.

I could tell that George was annoyed, but was too sleepy or maybe just not bright enough to know how to deal with the situation. Scratching himself and yawning, he flopped on to the soda.

'Don't knock yourself out, guys.' Ignoring Jade, he directed his words to us. 'My sis loves doing this stuff. It makes her feel like she's got a family. She can be Mom. Ain't that right, babe?'

'Can it, George,' said Jade quietly.

'Hey, attitude, sis.' George's smile had gone. 'Get us a beer from the fridge, will you?'

Jade was moving towards the kitchen when something seemed to snap in Wiki.

'No!' It was like a bark.

'It doesn't matter, Wik,' said Jade.

Wiki stood in front of her. He walked slowly to the

fridge, and took out a can. He made his way to George and stood over him.

'You don't talk to your sister like that.' Wiki spoke in a low voice. The last time I had seen that look in his eye, he had just brought down the intruder at Hill Farm with the help of his catapult. 'She deserves politeness.'

'Hey, butt out, kid.' George sat up. 'She's my family, right? Not yours.'

'It doesn't mean she belongs to you.' This was Trix. 'She's not your servant.'

Brad emerged from his bedroom, barefoot in jeans. 'Hi, kids,' he said, yawning. He looked around, suddenly aware of the atmosphere. 'Did I interrupt something?'

BRAD HART

So then I get this speech – I mean, literally, a speech – from this little black guy with glasses about how we should or should not treat our little sister.

I glance at George. Like, am I dreaming all this?

'So if you want something done while we're here, ask Mark or me or Tim,' goes the kid. 'Just leave Jade alone.'

'Hey,' snapped George. 'Here's the way it goes around. It's really, really simple. It's my road or the high road. Tomorrow morning, you kids can take a hike.'

JADE

My heart was thumping. I couldn't believe that Wiki, and then the other two, had stood up to my brothers.

At last I managed to speak.

'George, if you do that, I'll have nowhere to go. I'll tell Mom that you threw me out. And how you're living your lives.'

A mean, sulky look settled on my brother's face. It was as if he were sixteen all over again.

Shrugging, he picked up the remote control and pointed it at the big TV screen that covered most of one wall.

Bad, bad timing. The early evening news had just started.

WIKI

You couldn't call either of Jade's brothers exactly razor sharp. Maybe their brains were never overactive. Maybe years of clubbing had killed off what few brain cells they had. Either way, as they stared at the TV that evening, it took a while for the information received by their ears or eyes to filter through to their brains.

Trix was the headline story. The police had revealed that someone had sent a T-shirt. The Welsh police had been alerted. Cut to a press conference. Trix's mother was there, weeping in front of the cameras.

We looked at each other, the same question forming in our minds. Hadn't she got the text?

Some video footage of Trix was shown as the story switched to the police hunt in Wales. There was something about her case being mentioned by the Prime Minister in the House of Commons. The Show Us You Care fund had passed the million mark. A poster showing Trix appeared on the screen.

'Hey.' Brad sat forward in his seat. 'Hey, Tim's on TV!'

'Whoa –' George shook his head and focused his eyes on the TV – 'it can't be Tim, dude. It's a chick. But hey, it does look really like Tim.'

Brad turned to Trix. 'Are you a chick, Tim?' he asked.

To my surprise, Trix actually laughed. Looking over her Ray-Bans, she said, 'I'm afraid so, guys. I'm a chick.'

'And now for the day's other news,' the newsreader was saying.

George switched off the TV with the remote.

'OK, everybody,' he said. 'I think the time has come for us to have a little talk.'

MARK

It was all over. I was sure of it. Jade's brothers hated us anyway. Now they had the power to destroy the whole plan.

I looked at the Trixter. She was good at thinking fast, but not this time. Wiki seemed to have found something really interesting to stare at on the floor.

Then Jade wandered over to the sofa and sat beside her older brother.

'We've got a proposal to make to you,' she said.

JADE

We were seriously busted but, as the news was playing, I came up with an idea. It was last-throw-of-the-dice time.

'That million pounds they were talking about on the news?' I smiled at George. He nodded suspiciously.

'It's going to be ours,' I said.

Interested now, Brad sat on the arm of the sofa.

'Yup,' I said. 'This is a heist, guys. In a few days' time, we're gonna be seriously loaded.'

Trix widened her eyes, unable to believe what she was hearing. Somehow, almost for the first time in her life, she managed to keep her mouth shut.

'It's a heist?' Brad smiled, almost like a little boy. 'Like a gang thing?'

WIKI

Jade nodded slowly, the cunning smile of a master criminal on her face. She was a great actress, that was for sure.

'Can't give you all the details, guys.' Jade dropped her voice. 'But I can tell you this. If you let us stay here until –' She actually winked at this point – 'the sting, we'll cut you in for three big ones.'

'Each?' asked George.

'Pounds or dollars?' asked Brad.

Jade made a bit of a show of turning to Trix, then Mark, then me.

'Here's what we can do,' she said eventually. 'It's three hundred thousand between you. Dollars, not pounds.'

Brad gave a little giggle. 'That's a *lot* of party money.'

'And all you've got to do is keep quiet. It'll be the easiest money you've ever earned.'

'It'll be the *only* money we've ever earned,' said George.

'Deal?' asked Jade, holding out her hand.

Eagerly George, then Brad, shook their sister's hand.

As I say, not exactly razor sharp. They went back to their rooms to get dressed.

'Cool work, Jade,' said Mark.

'You did brilliantly,' I said.

There was a disapproving sniff from Trix's direction. 'I'm shocked,' she said, pursing her lips. 'All those lies. It's a slippery slope once you start offering money to people. But at least we're still standing.' A smile broke out on her face. 'All thanks to the Jadester.'

HOLLY

Early next morning, I received a call from Wiki.

'We need your help,' he said in that surprisingly confident tone of his.

'Now there's a change,' I said.

'Yesterday Trix sent her mother a text saying she was safe. Is there any way you could check whether she received it?'

'Wiki, how am I going to do that without giving the whole thing away?'

'Maybe that has to happen. The important thing is that Trix hasn't upset her mum.'

I sighed and was about to object but the new tough-guy Wiki was too quick for me.

'Do it for Trix,' he said, and hung up.

EVA JOHANSSON

You know that saying 'The show must go on'? It is very wise and true.

The morning after my appearance at the press conference, it was my face that appeared on the front page of many of the newspapers. 'MOTHER COURAGE' was the way one headline read. In one of the articles about the case I was described as *Eva Johansson, the brave and glamorous mother of Tragic Trixie.* It was almost embarrassing how much the newspapers loved me.

Late that night Eddison Vogel confirmed that I was to be crowned Share Celebrity Mother of the Year at the Grosvenor House Hotel at Sunday night's awards ceremony. I felt profoundly humbled.

'This is not about me,' I told Eddison. 'It's all about my darling Trixie. We must make that point.'

'Sure it is, babe,' he said.

I decided to wear a black Armani dress which had never been seen in public before.

EDDISON VOGEL

It was going to be a moving occasion. I had visualized it all. Eva making the speech about Trixie my people had written for her. The camera paning around the tables. A tear in Madonna's eye. Tom Cruise's bottom lip trembling. The member of the royal family (we're hoping it's Prince William) reaching for his handkerchief and wiping his nose in a moved but masculine way. Famous? Sure. Rich? Probably. But, deep down, celebrities and ordinary people are the same. We're human, and right now we're grieving for Tragic Trixie.

Eva would have one of the top tables where the TV cameras are trained throughout the evening.

But we wouldn't have celebrities. We would have good ordinary people from Trixie's life. The teacher from her school, her little friend Holly and Detective Inspector Barry Cartwright. We'd probably have to get the drunken dad along too, as long as we keep an eye on his glass.

It was going to be a beautiful occasion.

HOLLY

Here we go again. The other four were out there on some mad adventure and it was me – ever-dependable Holly – who was alone in the enemy camp, having to lie every time I spoke. It was the story of my life – others get the fun, I get the responsibility.

And now I had been given the job of finding out whether Eva Johansson, a woman I hardly knew, had received a text, and then reassure her that her darling Trix was safe – all without blowing the whole plan wide open.

I was trying to work out how I was going to get to Eva when Eddison Vogel rang me on my mobile.

EDDISON VOGEL

'Holly, love,' I said, 'cancel your plans for tomorrow night. You've been invited to join an international celebrity audience for the live, televised Share Awards. You can bring your mother with you if you want.'

'But why – ?'

I laughed lightly. I really was rather too busy to deal with questions from a schoolgirl.

'I can't explain now,' I said. 'Suffice to say, this is all for Trixie. We need to publicize the case. And there will be a small award for her mother. All very confidential, of course. Now, Holly, you can help me. Which teachers from Cathcart College should be invited?'

'Miss Fothergill, I guess. And maybe the headmaster, Mr Griffiths.'

'Great, great. And what about Trixie's friend Jade Hart? Where would I find her?'

HOLLY

Ah. Maybe I should have seen that one coming.

Vogel was asking for Jade's number. Panicking, I made one up. Then, taking a deep breath, I said, 'Is Eva there?'

'She's a very busy woman, Holly.'

'And this is very important,' I said.

Trix's mum came on the line. 'Holly?' She spoke with a croaky, suffering-mum voice, which seemed to come and go. 'How are you, love?'

'I'm fine, thank you. I was wondering whether you received a text yesterday.'

'Text?' The voice sounded faint.

'From Trix. Saying that she was all right – that you shouldn't worry about her?'

There was a long, long silence. When she spoke her voice was quiet and hard.

'Tell me about this on Monday morning,' she said. 'Let's deal with these awards first.'

For a moment I was unable to understand what she was telling me. Then I did.

Vogel was back on the line. 'All right, Holly? My assistant will ring with the details of tomorrow night later, hm?'

And he was gone.

EDDISON VOGEL

I could tell something was up. Eva had gone deathly white.

'Eddison,' she said, 'I've got a teeny-weeny confession to make.'

EVA JOHANSSON

I have a motto. It is: Honesty is the best policy. So now I spilt the beans, big time. I told Eddison about the text in the middle of the night, which I had thought was maybe a dream, but now I realized perhaps wasn't. I even mentioned the business about having had a secret cosmetic procedure done to the lower half of my body.

He frowned and glanced downwards and sideways at my figure.

'You had a buttock lift, babe?'

I nodded guiltily.

He glanced down. 'Good job,' he said. 'You must give me the name of your surgeon when this is all over.'

'What about the Share Awards? If Trix is out there, sending me texts about my bottom, it won't look good at the Share Awards, will it?

'Not great,' he said. He thought for a moment, then said, 'You were right. We'll deal with this on Monday.'

I smiled with relief. 'And we keep silent about my procedure?'

'As the grave, babe.' Eddison winked. 'As the grave.'

THE SMILER

Now we were cooking with gas. I had discovered that the great kidnap had never happened. It was just a bunch of kids on same crazy stunt of their own. Somehow they had managed to fool the police, their parents – the whole world, in fact, except for one person.

Unfortunately for them, that person was the Smiler.

I was one happy bunny. The kids had done my work for me. Now all I had to do was take possession of the merchandise and hold out for a big, fat ransom.

It took less than twelve hours for my good friend at the Vehicle-Licensing Authority to discover the details of the Porsche, registration number GR8 HARTS.

It was owned by a Mr George Hart of Lexington House, Curzon Street, London.

I grabbed my keys and jumped in the Discovery.

Watch out, Tragic Trixie. The Smiler is on his way.

WIKI

I took the call from Holly. We kept it short for security reasons. When I had hung up, I went to see Trix, who was in the kitchen with Mark.

'The good news is your mum got the message,' I said. 'Holly's spoken to her. She knows you're safe.'

'And the bad?'

'There's this big celebrity event tomorrow night. Your mother's going to be given some kind of award. She told Holly she didn't want to know anything until Monday morning.'

It seemed to take a moment for Trix to process this news. Then she began to nod thoughtfully.

'This is good,' she said. 'We know where we stand. Now we just have to decide how to use the information.'

It was Mark who expressed the thought that was on both our minds.

'But, Trixter, your mum is putting this celebrity thing before you. Isn't that rather weird?'

Trix smiled sadly. 'You know what one of my mother's favourite phrases is? "Hey, that's showbiz."'

She stood up, as if she had suddenly thought of something she had to do in her room.

Mark and I looked at one another. 'What a family,' he murmured.

DETECTIVE INSPECTOR BARRY CARTWRIGHT

Policing is all about teamwork. As the operation to find Trixie Bell proceeded, the officers involved in the investigation took on different roles. I was the frontman, dealing with the press (and even a film producer who seemed to think that yours truly had the makings of a film star!), while others did the all-important legwork.

So when Mr Bell came up with what he called 'a lead', involving a criminal he had allegedly exposed in the past and who very allegedly might have a grudge against him, I handed it over to one of my younger colleagues, Detective Constable Julie Summers. Like many women police officers, she was very good at dealing with members of the public who were finding the pressure of police investigations all a bit too much.

DETECTIVE CONSTABLE JULIE SUMMERS

To me, what Pete Bell said made sense. I checked on the national crime records. Charles Prendergast had been questioned in connection with post-office raids across Wales over the past nine months, but no charge had stuck.

However, there was a report from a few days before that struck me as odd. His car had been found miles away from where he lived.

I rang Swindon nick and talked to the officer who had been on the desk. Funnily enough, he said, they had been talking about the case that very morning. A gentleman from the village had rung to see how the investigation was going. Investigation? they had said. Yes, said the gentleman, surely the man with the scar had told them. There had been teenagers in the big car. It was late at night. There was something strange about it.

A man with a scar? That had to be our man.

Within half an hour we had put out an alert for the Discovery and for its owner, Mr 'Smiler' Prendergast.

WIKI

There was a strange atmosphere in the flat that afternoon. Ever since it had become clear that her mother was playing some strange celebrity game which only she fully understood, Trix had been in her room.

When she finally emerged, it was early evening and the three of us were waiting for the news to come on TV.

She slumped down beside Jade and for a moment stared blankly at the screen.

'Are you all right there?' Jade asked.

Trix sighed. 'It's over,' she said. 'There's no way out of this.'

'We gave it our best shot,' said Mark.

'Yup.' Trix sighed and, surprisingly, smiled. 'But least we can go out in style, right?'

We switched off the TV and Trix told us her plan.

THE SMILER

There it was. The Porsche. GR8 HARTS. Parked in Curzon Street. Trouble was, Lexington House turned out to be a big fancy block of flats with a doorkeeper in the lobby. I settled to wait and to watch. I had the time.

The moment of revenge was coming. It was so close that I could almost taste it.

MARK

One other thing happened that evening. Jade's brother George tumbled out of his room soon after seven, scratching himself and yawning. When he saw us, he grinned.

'The gang,' he said, remembering the conversation we had had earlier. 'So when are Brad and I going to get that little jackpot you promised?'

'We've just been discussing that,' said Trix. 'The sting is on Sunday night.'

'The sting, I love it.' George stretched, then reached

into his back pocket and took out a fifty-pound note. He ambled over to where Jade was sitting and tossed the money in her direction. 'Go get us a takeaway, sis,' he said. 'I'm starved.'

Jade was just about to stand up when Wiki spoke.

'No,' he said.

'Hm?' The American looked down, frowning. 'You talking to me, schoolboy?'

'We've told you. She's your sister, not a slave,' said Wiki.

'Maybe you should get your own dinner,' said Trix. 'You're not pushing Jade around any more. Not while we're here.'

I stood up, my heart thumping. George and Brad may have spent their lives clubbing and sleeping, but they were big and strong. Wiki stood beside me, his hand on the catapult in his pocket.

'Hey, Brad,' George called over his shoulder. We stood in silence for a moment. The door to Brad's room opened.

'How ya goin'?' Brad croaked sleepily.

George turned towards his brother. We held our breath.

'Looks like we're eating out tonight,' he said and, with one last sneer in our direction, he left the room.

Five minutes later they were gone, and we began to relax.

'I've never seen anyone do that to my brothers,' Jade said quietly.

She looked at each of us and for the briefest moment it seemed as if she might be about to thank us. But she gave a little laugh. 'We're the weirdest gang on the planet.'

Wiki had taken the catapult from his pocket and was

turning it over in his hand. 'I really wanted to use this too,' he said.

Jade laughed. 'Schoolboy,' she said.

THE SMILER

You can tell a lot from the way a man walks. How strong he is. If he'll give grief in a barney. Whether he's got heart.

The boys who made their way from Lexington House to the Porsche were built all right, but their walk gave them away. It was a sort of rich-kid roll, like you might see on a tennis court or a golf course.

They were going to be easy.

MISS FOTHERGILL

The evening that I received a call from Eva Johansson, I believed, briefly, that she had good news of Trix.

But no, it was some grand dinner with film stars, celebrity chefs and TV newscasters. I was reluctant. I feel out of my depth on these occasions. Besides, it seemed somehow inappropriate to be having a party while poor Trix was missing.

'But, Miss Fothergill, that is the point,' said Trix's mother. 'This is all to help my daughter. The police believe that publicity will help bring her back to us.'

Then she started crying.

Reluctantly, I agreed.

MR 'GRIFFO' GRIFFITHS

As headteacher of Cathcart College, I have a duty of care for all Cathcartians. It was important to show the world that our school is not just good at exams and sport. We are a concerned institution. Under these circumstances, I accepted the invitation on behalf of Mrs Griffiths and myself to attend the Share Awards.

BRAD HART

George seemed kind of glum that evening. We took in a pizza and he told me about what had happened earlier.

'I dunno,' he said. 'Maybe we've been kinda rough on old Jade. She is our sister, after all.'

'And she's about to earn us three hundred grand,' I said.

Then we started talking about the clubs we were going to hit that night.

THE SMILER

The Porsche went up west. I followed. I'd get my chance some time that night. You know the old saying? Good things come to those who wait.

I sat outside a pizza house. Then they drove to a club. An hour later, they were out again. Another club. The streets were full of people. I found a parking bay. It was for the disabled. That made me laugh. There was going to be some disabling done that night, that was for sure.

DETECTIVE CONSTABLE JULIE SUMMERS

The traffic unit called in that night. Prendergast's vehicle had been identified, parked illegally in central London.

The task force moved into action.

V Day + 19

GEORGE HART

By the high standards of the Hart brothers, we were having a quiet night. We took in Amnesia. It was dead. We moved on to the Rigmarole. It was hot and heaving, wall-to-wall babe.

They knew us there. We slipped a waiter a tip and he gave us a table near the dance floor. We were soon sharing a bottle of champagne or three with a couple of chicks. Sorry, can't remember their names.

BRAD HART

It was around two in the morning when the four of us were interrupted.

Looming out of the darkness, there was this old guy in a T-shirt. His face, lit up by the flashing lights, had this mad ugly grin on it. Even before he spoke, we could tell that he didn't exactly fit in at the Rigmarole. In fact, he wouldn't have fitted in anywhere, except maybe in a horror movie.

He tapped one of the girls on the shoulder and, with a jerk of his head, shouted, 'Scram.'

She was only a little thing and looked kinda scared.

'And you,' he said to the other one. 'Go on – scarper, both of you.'

'Now wait a minute,' George shouted, but the girls had seen enough. They were out of there.

The goon sat down beside me. He took one of the girls' wine glasses and filled it full with champagne, which he threw back down his throat.

Then he took the empty glass and tapped it casually on the side of the table. The sound of breaking glass was lost in the noise.

He held the broken glass, its jagged edges upwards, in his fist.

'We're goin' home,' he said. 'Back to your place. Now.'

George gave him a full-on stare. 'We're going nowhere,' he said.

Almost before he had finished, the man lunged under the table with the broken glass. George gasped with shock and pain as it hit his hand.

The goon gave a little laugh. 'You were saying?'

George lifted his hand. It was pouring blood.

'Put it under the table,' said the man.

I reached into my back pocket and took out a roll of notes.

'There's no need to rob our place,' I said. 'There's nothing there. Take this.'

He looked down at the wad of fifty-pound notes. Then, with a little shrug, he took it and jammed it into his pocket.

'Money isn't everything,' he said. 'Let's go.'

'What do you want?' I asked.

The goon put his mouth close to my ear. 'Trixie,' he growled. 'I want Trixie Bell.'

THE SMILER

It was easy. Too easy. If I'd been dealing with a couple of real men, I'd have taken more care.

There was a pool of blood under the table. Soon it would be flowing on to the dance floor.

I jerked my head in the direction of the exit.

The long-haired one stood up but the one I had winged whimpered something about tidying up his hand. There was so much blood, he said, we'd get noticed on the way out. He'd get a paper towel from the washroom.

It made sense. I nodded.

'Try anything and your mate's dead,' I said.

He blundered off. Berk.

JADE

Picture the horror. I'm fast asleep when my cellphone rings. It's George and he's borderline hysterical.

'Get out of the flat,' he said. 'There's this guy. He's after your friend Trixie. We're on our way now.'

'What?' I sat up. 'George, what is this—?'

'Just go,' he said. 'Now!'

WIKI

Jade burst into our room. She told us about the call from her brother. From the tone of her voice, we knew it was serious.

It took five minutes to get ourselves together. Weirdly,

Trix was the most reluctant to go – particularly when we told her she had to dress up in my clothes and get into her boy-in-shades disguise again.

The four of us took the lift downstairs and let ourselves out on to the empty neon-lit street.

Trying to look as if it were the most natural thing in the world for four kids, one wearing dark glasses, to be on the streets of London in the early hours of the morning, we started walking.

'Where exactly are we going?' Mark asked.

'Somewhere. Anywhere. Not here,' I said.

GEORGE HART

My hand was throbbing. The man in the nightclub walked behind giving us directions. He made us get into the big SUV he had parked nearby.

He made Brad drive, sitting in the back with me, the broken glass held against my neck.

We drove home, pulled up outside Lexington House.

We walked into the house, nodding to Bert, the night concierge, then took the elevator. Brad unlocked the door. I prayed.

The apartment was empty.

'Where are they?' The goon went from one room to another. 'Where are they?'

When he came back to the sitting room, he walked towards us almost casually. Then he grabbed Brad by the hair so that he lost balance and fell to his knees.

'*Trixie!*' the man bellowed, holding the glass in front of Brad's face.

It was then that all hell broke lose.

DETECTIVE INSPECTOR BARRY CARTWRIGHT

My officers arrested three men in connection with the abduction of Trixie Bell at a Mayfair address in the early hours of the morning.

Later that night we announced that there had been a significant breakthrough in our investigations.

Unfortunately there was no sign of the child herself. We remained deeply concerned about her welfare.

WIKI

A big city at dead of night, we discovered, has a life of its own. Gangs of partygoers – loud, sometimes drunk, often dangerous – stagger blindly along the pavements. In every dark street something secret is going on. Cars drive by in a slow, cruisy way, pale faces peering out, combing the streets. Mark said they were minicabs looking for customers. We all pretended to believe him.

At first, as we walked heads down through the neon-lit streets, we talked about the call from George. I was suspicious. I thought he was angry about what had happened that evening and, after a couple of drinks, had decided to get us out of the flat.

'Maybe he was scared of being found out – of getting in trouble with the police,' said Mark.

Trix glanced in Jade's direction. 'So much for your family contacts,' she muttered.

Jade stopped walking.

'You guys kill me,' she said, her eyes blazing. 'You think you know people, each of you. Cool-guy Mark. Catapult-boy Will. The great Trixter herself. But you know nothing. You are beyond crapass when it comes to psychology.'

'We didn't mean to upset you,' said Trix.

'Here's a tip,' said Jade. 'Think. Use your eyes. Listen. My brothers may be kind of flaky but they haven't had parents, right? They've been on their own for as long as I remember.'

We stood in an embarrassed huddle, each of us wondering at the fact that we were actually being told off by Jade Hart.

'So get this,' she said quietly. 'My brothers don't lie. They just don't. You should be thanking them right now.'

She walked towards us and kept going, barging between Mark and me.

'Make like you're going somewhere,' she called over her shoulder. 'That way people will ignore us.'

She was right. We followed her, walking fast, Mark with a bag slung over his shoulder, Trix with a duvet rolled up under her arm. It was strange, but Jade's anger had given us strength.

We kept off the main streets, looking for some dark corner of the city where we could rest. We must have been going for about half an hour when, turning a corner, we saw what looked like a brightly lit shop. As we approached it we saw tables, a couple sitting inside.

We stopped and looked longingly towards it, like people lost in a desert who have just seen an oasis and are worrying that it might be a mirage.

But it was real all right. Over the door, in rickety orange

lights, were the words 'THE UP-ALL-NIGHT CAFE'.

TARIQ AMIN

We get all sorts in the Up-All-Night – taxi-drivers, couples, people who have nowhere to go, even kids sometimes. When these young teenagers, three boys and a girl, came in and sat at a table, I asked them why they were out so late. The three boys looked guilty and said nothing. It was the girl, an American, who answered.

JADE

The two boys were suddenly a word-free zone. Trix was doing her moody act behind her dark glasses. We were yay-close to getting well and truly busted.

It was time for my cute smile.

'We were at this party,' I said as brightly as I could manage. 'My father was meant to be taking us home but he never turned up. We've phoned him. Could we just wait here till he picks us up? It's kind of scary out there.'

The Asian guy, a small, tired-looking man, gave us this kind of suspicious sidelong look.

Then he said, 'So you'll be wanting breakfast then.'

WIKI

Jade saved us. I remembered what she had said, a few days

back, in another lifetime it seemed, when we were at Hill Farm. It was true. She *was* a good liar.

After she had made her little speech, even we believed her and kept looking out for the non-existent car that would be collecting us, driven by a father who was thousands of miles away.

We had a big breakfast, with cups of tea. We pretended to call Jade's dad on our mobile phones. Now and then the only other people in the Up-All-Night, a man and a woman in their thirties, glanced in our direction, but from the look of them they had other things on their minds.

For two hours, three, we stayed at the Up-All-Night, our eyes aching, our heads buzzing with tiredness. Soon after six thirty a man in a suit came in, ordered a coffee and sat at the next table. He was clean-shaven, sober, tidy – a man on his way to work.

'Here's what we're going to do now.' Trix spoke quietly. Those shades did something to change her character. She sounded like some Mafia gang leader. 'I'm calling Holly. She's going to get us into the Share Awards tonight. All we have to do is stay out of sight for the rest of today.'

'I could use some sleep,' murmured Mark.

'It'll be all over soon.'

DETECTIVE CONSTABLE JULIE SUMMERS

It was a long night but, by the time the next day dawned, we were no nearer the truth.

There were traces of the missing child's DNA in Prendergast's car and in the two Americans' flat. They were all telling us different stories, none of which stacked up.

Hours before, we had been hopeful. Now we began to fear the worst. We had the kidnappers, but where was Trixie?

HOLLY

It was early morning when my mobile vibrated softly under my pillow. The call was from Wiki. I sighed. More bad news, I supposed.

'Now what?' I said.

'Holly, listen carefully,' Wiki's voice sounded different – hoarse, tired. 'We're on the run. We're turning ourselves in tonight.'

'Wik, it's not even seven. What's going on?'

'Tell us where the Share Awards are.'

Grumbling, I got out of bed and walked to my dressing table, where I had left the invitation. 'The Grosvenor House Hotel on Park Lane,' I said. 'We're getting there at seven thirty tonight. The broadcast starts at eight thirty.'

'When will Trix's mum be on?'

'I don't know. How am I meant to know that?'

'OK, OK,' he said. 'There's just one thing you've got to do.'

I sighed. 'Go on then.'

'You've got to get us into the Grosvenor House for when Trix's mum is on stage.'

'*What?*'

'Just try, Holly. You can do it.'

'But how?'

'I've gotta go,' he said. 'Ring me back on this number when it's sorted.'

And he was gone.

I stumbled back to bed and tried to sleep. How did I end up being the gang member who has to do the tough stuff on her own?

MARK

It was a new day – a moment of maximum danger. The streets were full of people, and they weren't drunk.

We headed south, heads down, keeping to the small streets. Wiki seemed to think there would be more hiding places near the river.

'Er, why?' asked Jade.

'Bridges,' said Wiki, as if that explained everything. 'If you want to hide in London, bridges are a good place to start.'

Now how did he know that?

JADE

The river: there were no hiding places – just traffic and noise and a big brown River Thames flowing by, making us feel small and scared.

Nice work, Wiki.

'Maybe it's better on the other side,' he said.

'Let's go.' Trix marched ahead. The sun was high in the sky as we trudged, bone-weary, across Waterloo Bridge.

On the other side, we went down some steps to a path by the river. There were skateboarders clattering noisily nearby.

Mark walked over and asked them if there was anywhere we could get some sleep without being disturbed. The guy pointed downriver. There were warehouses down there, he said – storerooms. You could do all kinds of stuff without being discovered.

All we wanted to do was sleep. We stumbled on in silence, Trix leading the way. She had a talent for knowing when she had to be strong for all of us.

Ten minutes later we found somewhere dark, quiet and damp. It would do for now.

Wearily we laid our coats on the ground and sat on them. Trix covered the four of us with the duvet she had been carrying since we left the flat.

'Sleep,' murmured Mark.

'Ye'll be lucky,' said a voice from the darkness.

JAZ CORBY

I was resting a while after doing the South Bank run. There's good takings late at night by the river, with folk coming back from theatres and movies and the like, full of food and guilt. I had been too tired to walk home. Suddenly I had company. Kids – hardly older than me. I could tell they weren't from the streets. They talked too loud, for a start. And, besides, no one who knows their way around town would end up here.

WIKI

I gripped my catapult. Mark and I stood up slowly. Across the way was what we had thought was a pile of old rags. The voice, a hoarse, thin whisper, had come from that direction.

As we approached, it spoke again.

'Easy,' it said. 'I'll nae harm ye.'

There was a patch of white amidst the dark rags. A glint of light reflected in an eyeball revealed that it was a human face – pale, dirty, small.

'Ye'll nae sleep here,' he said. 'There's rats and all kindsa nasties come visitin' late at night.'

'D'you live here?' Mark asked.

'Ye're jokin', mon.' The face almost smiled. 'I got a nice place in the park. Proper peaceful, almost as good as a house. That's where I kip down normal like.'

A small hand emerged from the rags. The kid wiped his nose.

'Ye wanna see it?' he said. 'Ye can kip down there if ye like.'

We walked back to the girls. Something about the mention of rats helped us make the decision.

I walked back to the bundle. 'That would be good,' I said. 'We'll only be a few hours.'

'Ach, ye can stay as long as ye like.'

The kid rolled around a bit, chucked off his blankets and stood up. He was skinny and small – shorter even than Trix. As he expertly bundled his bedding into a large carrier bag, he said, 'I'm Jaz, by the way.'

'Jaz,' said Mark. 'Cool name.'

'Aye.' The kid sniffed and spat on the ground. 'Short for Jasmine.'

PETE BELL

I heard the story on the news before the police rang me.

That was how it was when Barry Cartwright was in charge. Publicity came first at all times.

After the first brief hit of hope came the slump of despair. Three men were involved, not just Prendergast. Trix was nowhere to be found. I looked through my records. Americans, Cartwright had said. There were no American contacts in the past of Smiler Prendergast. We had hit a brick wall.

JADE

Weird stuff. The skinny little kid who had scared the wits out of us turned out to be a girl. She was twelve and came from Glasgow.

Jaz chatted away about her life on the streets, now and then laughing crazily at the things that had happened to her. Trix asked her what she was doing, living on the streets of London.

'Ran away.' Jaz hunched her shoulders as if the weather had suddenly turned cold. 'Long story,' she said.

'And didn't they search for you?' asked Trix.

'Search for me?' Jaz laughed crazily 'They'll nae have noticed I'm even gone.'

HOLLY

It was time for action. I rang Eva Johansson.

'Hi, Eva,' I said. 'I was wondering if my cousin could come to the dinner tonight.'

'Oh, Holly. You know this is a big celebrity occasion.

We can't just get any old cousin along. The Prime Minister might be there. Now, I'm sorry, I'm very, very busy.'

I listened carefully, then asked, 'Is there someone I could ring to see if my cousin could be found a place on another table?'

Eva sighed loudly. 'You can try Gemma Mann. She's the TV producer's assistant.' She gave me the number. 'But, lovey, don't hold your breath, right?'

I said goodbye politely, then went to the mirror. I tried to get the expression on Eva Johansson's face – the warm, caring eyes, the public smile that was never far away, particularly when cameras were around.

'But, lovey, don't hold your breath, right?' I repeated her words and smiled. The voice was good. 'Oh, Holly,' I said with perfect Eva Johansson intonation. 'You know this is a big celebrity occasion.'

I took a deep breath and dialled the number she had given me.

When Gemma Mann picked up, I switched on the smile and moved into character.

'Hi, Gemma, it's Eva Johansson. Now, lovey, I have a little favour to ask of you.'

GEMMA MANN

I received a call from Eva Johansson on the morning of the Share Awards. It was panic stations, as usual. We had been setting up at the Grosvenor House since seven in the morning. I remember thinking that it was a slightly odd request, but in the celebrity business you get used to those.

A friend of the missing girl Trixie was a guest on their table and wanted to look around the Grosvenor House before the event.

Sure, sure. If the girl rang me that afternoon, I'd get someone at the hotel to show her around.

'Oh and, lovey, there was one other thing.' Wincing, I glanced at my watch. This was frankly all I needed.

'I need to know exactly when the Share Celebrity Mother of the Year Award will take place. I like to be ready, you know – even if I'm ready to be completely surprised.'

There was no need to look at the schedule. By now I dreamed this stuff. 'You're on at nine fifty-two p.m., Eva,' I said.

'Thank you, Gemma darling.'

Problem solved. Next!

WIKI

That morning we discovered another world, hidden in the heart of the city.

Jaz took us to what she called her home. Walking with her, we no longer skulked down the dark backstreets. We walked chatting loudly down the wide pavements of the main roads. It was as if, because Jaz was there, we owned the streets.

At first we were scared that someone would recognize Trix, even behind her dark glasses, but soon we realized there was no danger of that. To the people hurrying by – people with houses and jobs and busy, busy lives – we were invisible. They didn't see us because they didn't want to see us.

We came to some grass – more like a bit of forgotten scrubland than a park. Laughing, Jaz said it was her garden. Beyond what had once been a toilet block but was now chained shut, were some small trees and bushes.

Jaz gave a low whistle as she pushed her way through some branches on to an overgrown path. Beyond a big oak was a clearing. Dotted around were what looked at first like some old sheets thrown over piles of rubbish. Then we saw that they were bits of odd plastic sheeting and tarpaulins, fixed and tied to the bushes.

We were in a camp.

'The others will be away workin' – tappin', like. They'll be back later, right enough.'

She took us to a corner of the camp where an old car cover had been strung between two branches.

Jaz gave a little speech. 'Welcome,' she said in the poshest English accent she could manage, 'to my little home.'

JADE

Where Jaz lived: let's just not talk about it. We made polite noises – 'So cosy,' said Mark, which was kind of pushing it in my view – but I guarantee we all had the same thought in our heads.

How could anyone, let alone a kid, live here?

On the other hand, we were shattered after a whole night without sleep.

Without a word, Trix threw the duvet she had been carrying around with her on to the ground and collapsed on it. I sat beside her. There was just enough room for the boys.

Jaz unrolled her blanket and lay it over the four of us. I decided not to comment on the smell.

'Time for a kip,' she said.

The sun was warm. The birds were singing. The roar of traffic grew fainter. We kipped.

THE SMILER

'There's been a terrible misunderstanding, officer.'

I'll be honest, I've said those words a few times in my life and they have not been entirely true.

But now they were.

'There's been this terrible, terrible misunderstanding,' I told the numbskull detective – Cartwright was his name – who questioned me through the night.

'Yeah, right, Smiler,' he said. 'Now why don't you tell us where the girl is?'

BRAD HART

My brother and I are not strangers to the British cops. There have been one or two incidents – drink-driving, that kind of thing. But this was different.

I told them we were not kidnappers. I told them everything. I asked them to check with George, who was being interviewed separately. I gave a load of telephone numbers.

An hour later, the cop was back. They had rung Jade.

She wasn't picking up. They had rung my mom. Whatever she was doing in Barbados with her barman, she wasn't taking calls either. They had even spoken to Mr Hart in Vegas. He swore at them and said he had nothing to do with what his sons were doing.

So the questions started all over again. Thanks, Jade. Thanks a bunch.

DETECTIVE INSPECTOR BARRY CARTWRIGHT

Here's where the investigation stood that afternoon. We had in custody a well-known criminal and two American youths. We could find no connection between the criminal and the wastrels, yet all three of them knew more than they were saying. There were DNA traces of Trixie in Prendergast's vehicle, in the Porsche of the Hart brothers and in their flat. We had also found items of children's clothing, female and male, at the same address.

There was one lead. All three suspects talked about a group of children. The Americans actually claimed that Tragic Trixie was involved in the kidnap herself.

Clearly that was a nonsense, but I began to wonder whether there was not some kind of teenage-gang thing going on.

Kid kidnappers? I tell you, these days anything is possible.

MARK

Trix woke first. She sat up sharply with a little gasp.

'You all right, Trix?' Jade asked.

'I dreamed of my father,' she said. 'He was in this lighthouse, trapped. I couldn't get to him.'

The only times the Trixter had mentioned her dad, she had said that he had a serious drink problem.

'I've got to call him,' she said. 'Tell him I'm OK.'

'Trix, he'll find out tonight,' said Wiki.

'You always said we shouldn't trust adults to keep quiet,' I said. 'He'll go to the police.'

We should have saved our breath. The Trixter does not change her mind. Never did. Never will.

PETE BELL

I thought it was Cartwright. He had rung me twice during the morning, keeping me up to date with the increasingly confusing progress of their investigation. But it wasn't.

When I first heard Trix's voice, it was as if I had been hit by this wave of fear and nausea.

'Dad, it's Trix.' She spoke slowly. 'I'm all right. Do you understand? I'm all right. It's a long story. I'll tell you later.'

'I've been worried. The nation has been looking for you. I think you'd better tell me now.'

She told me.

At first I was angry. Then, as she told me about Africa and the village she hoped to save, it began to dawn on me that quite possibly I have the craziest, most idealistic, most adorable daughter in the world.

'Dad –' She lowered her voice – 'do you promise not to give us away before tonight?'

241

What could I do? I promised.

It was only after I had hung up that the tears began to come.

EVA JOHANSSON

I was crazy busy that day. The hairdresser, the stylist, the personal trainer, the dresser – they all wanted a part of me before I took centre stage at that evening's Share Awards.

Yes, I could have gone looking like an ordinary mum. But I was to be the Celebrity Mother of the Year. The whole point of being a celebrity is that we don't look ordinary. We owe it to our public to be special.

Then there was the detective, Cartwright. Suddenly he was excited. He had some men in custody. He had leads.

'Excellent, Barry,' I said, as my hair was styled, my hands manicured, my legs waxed. 'Now, can we talk about this later? Maybe over dinner?'

DETECTIVE INSPECTOR BARRY CARTWRIGHT

I considered the option of not attending the glittering international celebrity event at the Grosvenor House that evening, and discussed it with senior members of my team. In the end, I decided that, for reasons of profile and publicity, it was important that the police – that is, myself – should be present. I would, in fact, be wearing uniform.

There's nothing the press photographers like better than a nice uniform.

WIKI

Late that afternoon, we met Cath and Rob, a couple in their twenties who lived in the camp. At first they were wary of us, but Jaz told them that we were on the run like she was.

They were fine, Cath and Rob. It turned out that they had just been to the yard behind a local supermarket, where the food that has reached its sell-by date is thrown out.

'Yay! Picnic!' said Jaz.

We unloaded the bags, put the containers of food on the grass, and tucked in.

I swear, it was the best meal I have ever had.

JADE

We were sampling the delights of life on the street when my cellphone rang. It was Holly.

'OK, gang.' She spoke in a low, urgent voice. 'I'm outside the Grosvenor House Hotel and I've got to be quick. I've checked out the place. There's a fire door on the ground floor, which leads to a street around the back of the building called Park Street. Trix's mum gets her award at nine fifty-two. I'll be at the fire door to let you in at nine forty-five. Got that?'

'Got it.'

'And be there on time. The place will be crawling with security people.'

'How will—'

'Got to go,' she said. 'My mum's coming.'

'Thanks, Holly. I don't know how you did it, but thanks.'

I was talking to myself. She was gone.

'OK.' I turned to the others. 'We should make a move.'

'We'd better find out how to get there,' said Mark. 'I've never been to the Grosvenor House Hotel before.'

'Nae problem.' Jaz stood up. 'I've worked the ol' Grosvenor House many a time. I'll take ye there.'

'Jaz.' It was Trix and she was speaking quietly. 'You are my hero.'

WIKI

We were like the unit of some secret army. We walked quickly through the streets of London. There was no looking around to see whether any of us had been recognized. It was too late for that now.

We were on our way.

MARK

Nobody talked. That's what I remember. Each of us thinking of what had been and what was ahead. Even Jaz seemed to understand that it wasn't the moment for conversation.

In a couple of hours it would all be over. The question was no longer whether we were *in* the doo-doo, but how deep.

JADE

Now and then, as we walked, I glanced at Trix. She was behind Jaz, between Wiki and Mark in front of me. It was as if she were some great leader and we were her bodyguards.

Leader? Excuse me, how did that happen?

WIKI

One moment we were walking through the city on just another night, the next police were everywhere.

A big crowd was gathering outside the Grosvenor House, where metal barriers had been erected to allow celebrity guests to walk up the red carpet without having to get too close to ordinary people.

We walked past the front entrance towards the small street that led to the back entrance where Holly was going to get us in.

We stopped. A line of uniformed policemen blocked the way.

EDDISON VOGEL

I have been to many, many awards ceremonies around the world, but the Share Awards were always very special. They were not about who was the best actor or the most success-ful model, but something very much more important.

They celebrated being human. For me, that's the biggest prize of all.

The fact that, after she was crowned Share Celebrity

Mother of the Year, Eva would never have to look for work again, that I would be acknowledged as one of the great personal publicists of recent (possibly all) time, was a bonus, but that evening was no time to talk about money or fame.

It was caring for other human beings, not being successful, that mattered.

EVA JOHANSSON

I was in the zone. When the limousine arrived, I stepped out, followed by Eddison. The cameras flashed. There was a rustle of recognition among the fans. A few applauded. Other celebrities would be greeted with more noise and excitement, but I was, I realized, a special case – famous, yet also a grieving mother.

I walked the red carpet. The reception was dignified. I felt warmed by the buzz of interest, the flash and whirr of cameras. It was all going to be fine.

Gemma Mann greeted us.

'Did you find a place for the cousin of Trixie's little friend Holly?' I asked as we entered the dining room.

'Cousin?' she said.

PETE BELL

What a circus. I hadn't worn a dinner jacket and bow tie for years. The jacket was too tight, the shirt was strangling me.

When I arrived at the Grosvenor House, I showed my

invitation to the security guard and, for the first time in my life, I walked the red carpet.

No one noticed. The Share Awards are unusual in that celebrities mix with what the famous call 'civilians' – people like teachers, nurses and social workers, who do ordinary jobs. Celebrity? Civilian? The photographers needed one look at me to see where I belonged.

I walked into the ballroom, where ordinary folk like me were looking for their places among the mass of circular tables. It was an amazing sight – chandeliers, glitter and, at one end of the room, the stage where the presentations would take place.

A distant voice urged us to take our places. I found our table. Eva and the little creep Vogel were already there. So were Holly and her mother, a couple I later discovered were teachers from Cathcart College and, to my surprise (hadn't they got better things to do?), Detective Inspector Barry Cartwright and Detective Constable Julie Summers.

There were still a few empty seats at the best tables. It was where the celebrities would be sitting. They are brought in at the last minute on these occasions, as if they are afraid of catching ordinariness from the other diners.

I sat down beside one of the teachers, who turned out to be called Helen Fothergill. She told me she had greatly admired my daughter.

That, I thought to myself, might be just about to change.

HOLLY

My mum and I were among the first to be in the ballroom.

Even when it was half empty, it was like a scene out of some strange dream – the dark, low-ceilinged room, the glitter, the lights, the brand placements. Somehow everyone looked slightly better than they would normally. It was as if we were all celebrities for the night.

Even Trix's father looked quite good when he turned up on his own. Trix never talked much about him and, when she did, it was with embarrassment, but he seemed like a normal dad to me, looking about him, then raising his eyebrows at me as if to say, 'What are we doing here?' There were bottles of wine on the table, but he poured himself a glass of water and drank deeply. So much for the drunk dad, I thought.

Something else. He looked, I don't know, cheerful. Pretending to look at the menu, I sneaked another glance at him. There was no doubt about it. The little smile on his lips gave him away. I was sure of it now. Pete Bell knew.

JADE

Hm. Problem. A line of uniformed policemen stood between us and the Grosvenor House.

The five of us hovered in the shadows. I glanced at our gang. We were all thinking the same thing.

'We're buckled,' said Mark. 'No way are we going to get past them.'

'Maybe we can get through the front entrance,' said Wiki.

'Forget it,' snapped Trix. 'You saw the security there.'

Wiki reached into his back pocket and took out his favourite weapon.

248

'Don't even think about it, Catapult Boy,' I said.

Trix took off her dark glasses and rubbed her eyes wearily.

'We'll turn ourselves in tomorrow,' she said, back in commander-in-chief mode. 'This isn't going to work.'

We stood in silence, each of us aware that none of us actually knew what Trix was planning to do once she got into the awards.

'I just wanted to talk to people,' she said quietly. 'I wanted to explain.'

'Maybe it's better if we're not on TV,' said Wiki unconvincingly.

'Ye're kiddin, mon.' The voice was an angry squawk from behind us. 'Ye're nae bottlin' it at this stage.'

Jaz. For a moment, we had forgotten about her.

'Have you got a better idea?' Wiki asked rather coldly.

'Aye,' said Jaz. 'I have, as it goes.'

HOLLY

The famous don't wait. The rest of us had been sitting around for half an hour or so when out of the shadows, like ghosts with very familiar faces, the guests of honour were escorted to their seats. It was all done coolly and naturally, as if anyone who happened to be a film star or a face from TV had been held up in traffic. One moment there were gaps on each table, the next there were celebrities everywhere. It was surreal.

A woman came on to the stage and, with some difficulty, managed to quieten down the conversation. She told us that the Share Awards would shortly be going out live. We should switch off our mobile phones. The award-winners should keep their thanks short. It was important that members of the audience, if they had to move, should do so while one of the little films were being shown.

The TV lights came on. Three huge photographs – of an old man sitting on a doorstep, of a woman in a wheelchair with a dog, and of a big-eyed African child – were lit up at the back of the stage. And then we were live, on air, on TV.

A large man with a face like a full moon appeared from the side of the stage. A wave of applause spread through the ballroom. I was just thinking that he looked a bit like Stephen Fry when he said, 'Hello, I'm Stephen Fry.'

MISS FOTHERGILL

It was all rather marvellous. Ordinary people who had done something rather brave or generous were greeted on stage by a series of famous faces. Videos were shown of the award-winners at work. There was applause and laughter and one or two tears. Throughout it all, I wondered what poor Trix would make of it all – not just the glamour, but the strangeness of the brave, small lives being celebrated as if they were successful films or performances.

Once or twice I tried to catch Holly's eye. She seemed surprisingly uninterested in the Share Awards – almost distracted. She kept looking at her watch as if she had an urgent appointment somewhere else.

Girls, honestly! You can never quite predict how they are going to behave.

HOLLY

The stars appeared on stage, one after another, to give out awards. There was a woman who had fostered about a million children, then a doctor who rescued a child from a cliff ledge, then someone who had campaigned for a hospital, then a teacher, then a kid in a wheelchair. Tears, cheers, hugs.

For me it was all background noise. Time crawled along like a slug on Valium. There was a clock on the wall behind Eva Johansson. I looked at it, then checked my watch. Neither seemed to be moving at all.

Then at last Stephen Fry announced the award for the Share World Poverty Campaigner of the Year. Eva would be next. It was nine forty.

My mouth was dry. I felt sick with fear.

'I'm not feeling too good,' I murmured to my mum.

'*Darling?*' She put on her concerned face. 'Can you just hold on for a few minutes?'

A film about the well-known stand-up comedian and his work for poverty was on the screen. It was now or never.

'I'll be right back,' I said and, before anyone could speak, I was off my seat and, looking neither to the left nor the right, I scurried towards the exit.

A security man opened the door and for a moment the strip lighting outside blinded me.

'Is everything all right?' A woman with a clipboard advanced towards me.

'Fine,' I said.

I kept walking.

We were in a doorway some twenty metres from the line of policemen, who had relaxed now that the show had started. There were eight of them there, standing in a group, chatting.

Our eyes were fixed on the door beyond them. At any moment now, Jaz would be doing whatever she could to divert their attention. There would be seconds to slip past them to the door.

'Two minutes to go,' I murmured. 'Everyone OK?'

'As if,' said Jade.

'Ready as I'm ever going to be,' Mark muttered.

I looked around for Trix. There was no sign of her. I walked away from the others and caught sight of a small figure standing in a side street some twenty metres from where we stood. Its head was down, as if it were examining something on the pavement.

'Trix?' I said the word out loud and began walking quickly towards her.

When I reached her, I put a hand on her shoulder. There was no reaction. 'Are you all right, Trix? It's time to go.'

She sniffed and looked up at me. Her eyes were dark and shining.

'What is it?' I asked.

She shook her head silently.

'Hey, this is going to be nothing compared to what we've been through.'

She closed her eyes, not bothering to wipe away the tears which spilt on to her cheeks.

'You can do it,' I whispered. 'Come on. You're the Trixter.'

'It's over,' she said.

'Maybe we didn't get the money but—'

'I didn't mean that.' Her voice was so low that I had to lean towards her to catch what she was saying. 'I was thinking of what we've been through together.'

I glanced back towards Mark and Jade. They were looking anxiously in my direction. Beside them, Jaz seemed to be doing weird little warm-up exercises.

'Trix, let's talk about this later,' I said.

'It'll be finished then.' She smiled sadly, as if she really had gone mad. 'We'll be back in the real, regular world.'

I looked at my watch. Nine forty-four.

'It was great being free, wasn't it?' Trix looked into my eyes as if desperate to make me understand. 'We were doing something. No school, no parents, just us. We took control. We changed things and then . . . things changed us. D'you remember that time when—'

There was a wild scream from behind us. We both looked round to see Jaz dancing crazily in the direction of the police, warbling as she went. She waved her carrier bag around like a magician about to do a trick.

'Come on!' I grabbed Trix by the T-shirt and we began running.

By the time we reached Jade and Mark, the police had noticed Jaz. There was a heavy litter bin just short of where they stood. She looked into it, her head almost disappearing. The police stopped talking and stared.

While scrabbling around, throwing newspapers and bits of litter over her shoulder, she reached into a pocket and took something out. Seconds later, the newspapers in the bin were alight.

'Agh! Agh! Aaagghhh!'

Jaz staggered back, holding a blazing newspaper.

'Her clothes!' gasped Jade. 'They'll catch fire!'

The policemen were thinking the same thing. As one, they rushed over to the tiny, turning, screaming figure.

'Time to go,' I said.

Jade's eyes were still on the burning figure. 'What about—'

Trix grabbed her arm. 'She's OK!'

In single file, at a fast walk, we made our way past the police who were trying to restrain a hysterical Jaz.

We turned into Warwick Street. There was a small door marked 'NO ENTRY'. Mark hammered on it with the heel of his hand. It opened.

Holly was there in her evening dress. 'What kept you guys?' she asked.

'It's a long story,' I said.

JAZ

I've done the old fire-dance trick loads of times before. It's no big deal, but it's a show-stopper every time. As the busies tried to restrain me, I saw the guys slipping past us. But I kept on fighting right enough – just for fun.

EVA JOHANSSON

Eddison, who knows about these celebrity things, told me I had to look shocked and surprised when the announcement was made.

'Remember that you're not expecting anything, Eva,' he said. 'You're just an ordinary mum doing her best in a terrible situation.'

The award before mine was handed over. Applause. Sir Richard Branson was invited on to the stage. My palms were sweaty. I could hardly breathe.

Shocked. Surprised. Not expecting anything. I am just an ordinary mum. That was all I had to remember.

SIR RICHARD BRANSON

There is nothing more important in my view than motherhood. I mean, without mothers where would we be? Literally, nowhere. I know that, at Virgin, some of the most dynamic people are the mums we have working for us. So for me, and for everyone working with me at Virgin, it was a great honour to be asked by Share, one of my very favourite charities, to present the Celebrity Mother of the Year Award to Eva Johansson.

HOLLY

Don't get me wrong but they looked terrible. I had just spent an evening in the world of celebrities, where everyone is lovely and quite a lot of them are beautiful. But when Trix, Jade and the two boys came towards me, I thought I was about to be mugged by a gang of child beggars.

And they were kind of smelly too. Jade and Trix hugged me (My dress! Mind my hair!) and I caught a definite whiff of the streets from them.

But it was too late to worry about that.

'Follow me,' I said.

PETE BELL

If anything was going to send me back to the bottle, it was watching my ex-wife pretending to be surprised when Sir Richard Branson opened the golden envelope and read out her name.

For some reason, something Trix used to say suddenly came back to me at that moment.

Please, *spare* me.

EVA JOHANSSON

Oh. Ah. I don't believe it. It can't be true. Me? *Me? ME????* But I'm just an ordinary mum! I'm confused. What should I do now? Go up on stage? Get an award? Me? Oh. Oh, this is all too much.

HOLLY

This was the bit that had worried me throughout the day. I had left the ballroom five minutes ago. Now I needed to get back in. Oh, and there were four street urchins behind me.

The woman with the clipboard was watching the TV pictures on a small monitor when she spotted us. She stood up, barring our way.

'Could I go back in, please?'

'We're on air,' she said. 'Who are these people?'

'They're friends. They wanted to . . . watch how the programme was made.'

MARK

On the screen behind the woman, the camera was on a spotlit figure making her way slowly towards the stage. It was Trix's mother.

'We've got to get on now,' I said loudly. 'This is really, really urgent.'

The woman pressed a small earpiece she was wearing. 'Security to ballroom entrance, please. We have intruders.'

Trix's mother was on the stage, standing behind a long-haired guy with a beard. She seemed unable to speak.

Someone pushed between me and Wiki.

It was Trix. She took off her dark glasses. 'My name is Trix. You know me as Trixie Bell,' she said. 'I demand to see my mother.'

The woman swallowed hard. I could see panic in her eyes. Then she stepped back. 'Sorry, I didn't see you there,' she said.

GEMMA MANN

It was her all right. I could have stopped her, maybe I should have stopped her, but in those seconds my instinct as a professional kicked in.

As the kids pushed their way through the door to the ballroom, I spoke to my producer.

'Get a camera on the kids coming through the main entrance now,' I said.

MARGARET BAIRD

I thought Gemma had gone quite mad. 'Kids?' I said. 'What's going on?'

'It's Trixie Bell,' said Gemma. 'The kidnapped girl. She's back.'

I glanced at the monitors. Five small figures had appeared through the main door. One of them, a young girl, I recognized as having been on Eva Johansson's table. The other four looked like something the cat had brought in.

'Trixie?' I said. 'Tragic Trixie?'

I hung up before Gemma could answer. 'Camera fifteen. The kids in the doorway. Close-up.'

The camera picked out the faces of what seemed to be five children. There was no doubt about it. The smallest kid, short-haired, with her dark glasses pushed back on her head, was the one and only Trixie Bell.

It was unplanned. It was unscripted. But it was going to be great TV.

EVA JOHANSSON

Sir Richard embraced me. He said, 'We're all very proud of you.' I turned, my eyes welling with tears, to face the lights, the guests at the Share dinner, which included several major film stars, the millions of TV viewers, my public.

'There is only one person who matters in all this,' I managed to say. 'And that . . . is my darling Trixie.'

There was applause from around the room.

I was about to continue when I became aware, as the clapping died down, of another sound – a sort of rustle of gasps and whispers from the far end of the room. I thought I heard a scream.

PETE BELL

Eva hesitated and suddenly I realized that she had lost her audience. People were looking away from the stage towards the back of the room. I glanced up at the nearest monitor screen to our table.

A spotlight had caught five small figures standing in front of the main door, and they were on camera. As they began to move forward, the symphony of surprise grew louder.

JADE

Whoa. Major scary moment. We had been thinking so hard about how to get into the Grosvenor House that none of us had known what was going to happen when we got there.

We walked in and there were tables as far as the eye could see. The stage where Trix's mom was speaking was a long, long way ahead.

For a moment we froze, and it was then that a spotlight picked us out.

Someone – Mark, I think – said, 'Now what?'

Did I say none of us knew? Wrong.

'Here we go,' said Trix loudly.

She began the long walk through the tables towards the stage.

EVA JOHANSSON

I had prepared a speech, thanking Eddison, Barry and his police colleagues, Trix's friends. It was going to be very, very moving. But when I saw these people at the back of the room walking towards me and I noticed that the camera was not on me but them, I lost my concentration.

'Is there something – ?' I turned to Richard Branson. But he was staring at the monitor too.

PETE BELL

There was confusion on stage. Stephen Fry stepped up to a microphone. 'I'm hearing through my earpiece that we have a surprise guest tonight.' He peered into the darkness, shading his eyes from the lights.

The camera closed in on the five figures. I could see Holly there. There was one boy with long, floppy hair. Another, a black kid wearing spectacles, seemed to have some sort of catapult sticking out of the pocket of his jeans. There was a tall girl I recognized as Jade Hart.

And there, at the front, dark glasses pushed back on her head as if she were some cool tennis player or something, was Trix, my Trix.

I couldn't help it. I started laughing.

EVA JOHANSSON

It was the nightmare scenario – that was what I thought at the time. This was my moment – the moment of Eva Johansson, the Share Celebrity Mother of the Year – and a group of scruffy children was destroying it. Not even Stephen Fry could think of something to say.

'What's happening?' I asked. 'Would someone please explain what . . . what . . . ?'

The children were approaching the stage. Through the dazzle of the lights I was able to see them more clearly. I noticed Holly first. Then, was that Jade there too?

I looked more closely at the small figure who was at the front of the group.

The microphone caught my sudden inhalation of breath.

'Trix?' I managed to say.

One after the other, the children climbed the steps on to the stage.

'Trix!' I repeated, and held my arms out to welcome her.

At first the applause was uncertain, but it built and built until it was deafening.

WIKI

As we reached the stage, the man standing behind a lectern on one side said, 'Is this Little Trixie? By Jiminy, it *is* Little Trixie. Ladies and gentlemen, I have to tell you that not one whisper of this occurrence had reached us beforehand. This is truly spontaneous TV.'

He moved towards Trix, who was first on stage but, ignoring him, she kept walking towards her mother. For a moment they stood in front of one another and silence descended on the ballroom. Then, as if at a signal, they fell into each other's arms. Like a mighty wave approaching the shore, applause filled the room, growing louder and louder.

DETECTIVE INSPECTOR BARRY CARTWRIGHT

There was little doubt about it. The missing girl was there, on the stage. I nodded to Julie. 'Get the team here – fast!'

It is not often that a kidnap victim – an alleged kidnap victim – is found live on national television. I had to think on my feet. Whatever the reason for Little Trixie's sudden magical reappearance, it was a police matter.

Cameras or no cameras, I needed to get on that stage.

EDDISON VOGEL

Some people can deal with situations. Some can't. Eva belonged to the second category. I had no idea why Tragic Trixie was suddenly on the stage or how she got there. Frankly, it wasn't my problem.

All I knew was that I had a client who was on live TV and, any moment now, was going to crash and burn big time. No way was I going to let that happen.

MARGARET BAIRD

'Keep the cameras rolling,' I said. 'Even if we run over time, we stay on air. We need to catch this.'

MARK

Blinking through the lights, I saw that the diners near the back had got to their feet. Soon the whole place was standing, clapping. I glanced across at Jade, uncertain as to whether we should be joining in or taking a bow.

She was nodding her head like a puppet. She muttered to me, 'This is beyond weird, dude.'

JADE

Mark's stage grin was yay-close to being a grimace of panic. Wiki looked as if he were about to wet himself.

The applause slowly died. Eva Johansson released Trix. Dabbing her eyes, while still looking lovingly at her darling long-lost daughter, she spoke into the microphone.

'Trixie, darling,' she said.

'Trix, Mum,' Trix interrupted. 'You call me Trix. Remember?'

'Trix.' Eva looked to the audience, then back at her daughter. 'What can I say? So, so much has happened and I –' Briefly she was lost for words – 'Darling, did you hear that I'm now the Share Celebrity Mother of the Year?'

EDDISON VOGEL

I had to get to her before she committed career suicide. I told the security guard standing between me and the stage that I was Eva's publicist but he seemed to be deaf.

WIKI

When Trix's mum mentioned being the Share Celebrity Mother of the Year, the audience started applauding and then, as if the same thought – *what a very strange thing to mention at this moment* – had occurred to each of them at the same time, they stopped.

In the silence, she opened and closed her mouth without any words coming out. Then she managed, 'There are several people I must thank for helping me win this prestigious award.'

There were mutterings in the audience. Her daughter had just returned from being kidnapped and she still wanted to make a speech – about herself?

Trix tapped her mother's arm. Her mother kept talking. Trix gently took the microphone from her hand, smiled at her mother, then at us. She faced the audience, suddenly looking small in the middle of the stage.

'Thanks, Mum,' she said.

There was laughter. Some people clapped. Trix remained quiet until total silence had returned to the room.

'I think I owe you all an explanation,' she said.

JADE

Trix's big moment. The four of us stepped back from the front of the stage. We watched – and wondered.

Here's the truth: Trix was not as different from her mom as she liked to think. The cameras, the lights, all those eyes on her made her cooler, more confident, bigger even, than she ever was in everyday life.

I'll admit it. Trix Bell could be a royal pain in the butt sometimes but none of us could have done what she did that night.

WIKI

She did this dramatic pause, looking around the big ballroom.

'For the past few weeks you've been asking who kidnapped me,' she said. 'The answer is . . . I did.'

This time the audience didn't applaud.

'With my brave and brilliant friends, I kidnapped myself.' She turned to where we stood. For some reason, almost as if we were about to be presented with prizes, we were standing in a line with parade-ground neatness.

I smiled modestly, but when I looked through the lights I realized that no one was smiling back. Suddenly the air seemed rather cold.

'You'll want to know why.' Trix wandered to the far side of the stage and stood in front of the big illuminated photograph of the little African boy, staring wide-eyed at the camera. 'For him.'

She walked back to the centre of the stage. She had

them now. 'And for millions and millions of children like him who have had their childhoods stolen and who may not even live to be adults. A few weeks ago, at my school, I discovered that people are good at giving money when there are celebrities involved – but, when there's no publicity, they don't care. I decided to do something that would raise money. So I got myself kidnapped.'

PETE BELL

I've never known a silence like it. As Trix – this kid, my kid – spoke quietly into the microphone, the mood in the ballroom seemed to change minute by minute. Surprise. Relief. Shock. Disapproval. Then, as Trix started talking about African children, everyone was with her.

After an evening of celebrity caring, this was the real thing.

STEPHEN FRY

Frankly I was startled at the way the event had gone. Normally these occasions are run with the brutal efficiency of one of Mr Mussolini's trains, but now the script had been completely abandoned.

'Let her talk,' the producer kept saying into my earpiece. 'This is good, Stephen.'

It was a strange and oddly touching occasion.

SIR RICHARD BRANSON

Personally, I found it all very moving. There is nothing more important in my view than kids. I mean, without kids, where would we be? They are literally the future.

I'm not ashamed to say that my eyes filled with tears as Trixie talked about Africa. I was proud to be on the same stage as her.

EVA JOHANSSON

Very nice, darling. Lovely speech. Great to have you back.

But when was she going to mention my award?

WIKI

Where had all this stuff come from? I'll bet we were all thinking the same thing.

The last time we had heard Trix talking to an audience about Africa had been in what now felt like another lifetime, at the Cathcart Charity Challenge. She had seemed preachy, annoyingly bossy. Now she was different. She sounded humble and talked to us as if each of us knew the right thing to do and just needed to be reminded of our better selves.

I looked down the line of faces at Mark, Jade and Holly and I could see that, as Trix spoke, they had forgotten how tired they were, how hungry, how strange it was to be standing on a stage in front of hundreds of people in smart evening clothes. There was even – I swear I'm not inventing this – a tear in Mark's eye.

It was as if she had been thinking about this moment ever since the idea for The Vanish had occurred to her, as if everything that had happened to us had made her more certain about what she believed in.

'Yesterday we decided that we had gone far enough.' She shrugged and, for a second or two, seemed lost for words. 'We met someone who, although she's only twelve, is the bravest person I've ever met. Her name is Jaz and she lives –' Trix hesitated – 'She lives everywhere and nowhere. She lives on the street because she has no home.'

'You've probably walked past her as you've come out of a restaurant or gone for a taxi. She's part of city life – the part we prefer not to see, not to think about too much.'

I wondered where Jaz was now. At some police station, probably.

'So here is what I want to do,' said Trix. She sniffed in that way that she did when she had made up her mind to do something. 'I'm hoping that the money that was raised for me, for the Show Us You Care fund, can be divided between the village of Mwanduna in Mali and charities for homeless children like Jaz. I don't know how this can be done but you do, don't you? You're grown-ups. We've done our best. Now, please, it's your turn.'

And with that, Trix handed the microphone back to her mother and walked back to us. As she walked towards us through the crashing applause, we noticed that there were tears in her eyes. Holly and Jade hugged her. I caught Mark's eye. There was no way we were going to miss this moment. We joined the group hug.

Stephen Fry stepped forward as Sir Richard Branson guided Eva Johansson to the far side of the stage.

From what I could hear, Stephen Fry was telling viewers that the show was over. 'We have stayed on air to report on quite the best news that the Share Awards could bring you,' he said. 'Trixie Bell is back. And we hope that the fund set up in her name will go to help the hungry and the homeless.'

He turned to us. 'Thank you, Trix. Thank you, Trix's gang.' He faced the camera once more. 'Our gratitude to our celebrity audience. And, above all, thank you all for showing us that you care.'

JADE

As soon as we went off-air, it was mayhem. Trix's mum was in bits. Her dad came up on stage. There was a police guy trying to fight his way through. The little guy Eddison Vogel was dancing around in front of the stage like a mad film director.

Some instinct made the five of us close together into a circle like some wacko little football team before a game. Hands tugged at our shoulders. Adult voices called out our names.

But through the craziness, above the noise, I heard Trix's voice.

'We did it,' she was saying over and over again. 'We did it.'

Within minutes of the end of the awards the five of us, with Trix's mother and father and Mrs de Vriess, Holly's mum, were being taken by police officers through the back corridors of the Grosvenor House. Outside, waiting for us, were three police cars. Mark and I were put in the first one, Holly, her mother and Jade in the second, while Trix, her parents and the detective – I recognized him from his appearances on the news as Barry Cartwright – were in the third.

It was getting really late by the time we reached the brightly lit police station. We were gathered in one room and Barry Cartwright talked to us all. He looked different without his dark glasses on.

He told us that he was, of course, delighted to find that we were safe. He was glad that we had handed ourselves in, although the police had been aware of what had happened and had been about to make their move. 'This is a case of what we call self-kidnapping,' he said. He would be calling the parents who were not already here. In the meantime he would be taking statements from us all.

'Now?' said Mrs de Vriess. 'Couldn't it wait?'

'I should remind you,' said the detective in his best serious-policeman voice, 'that at this point in time we are talking about a criminal investigation.'

'No.' It was Trix's father, Pete, who spoke up. 'These children are exhausted. They need a night's sleep before you speak to them.'

Cartwright smiled coldly. 'Mr Bell, they may be children but they have evaded capture for the past three weeks. At the very least, they are guilty of wasting police time. If we let them go—'

'They'll be with responsible adults,' said Pete Bell. 'Unless you are laying criminal charges, they should be released into our care. And if you are arresting them, the media should be told.'

'The media?' Barry Cartwright seemed to wince.

'It won't look good,' said Mr Bell. 'Not after Trix's speech. In fact, it could look pretty bad. How exactly will you explain it to the press?'

As the detective hesitated, looking over his notes as if they contained the answer to this question, I saw a little smile flicker across Trix's face. It had taken time but at last her dad had come though.

Cartwright seemed to have reached a decision. 'You'll all be here by ten a.m. tomorrow morning. Is that understood?'

He turned to the woman police officer who stood beside him. 'Julie, contact the other parents,' he said.

JADE

Problemo. My parents were seriously absent. Brad and George were either still in police custody or had just been released. Either way, they were not exactly the flavour of the month with the boys in blue.

I noticed that Holly was looking at me, smiling.

'I think Jade's parents are abroad,' she said, then turned to her mother. 'Would it be all right if she stayed with us?'

'Of course,' said Mrs de Vriess. 'It's always a pleasure having Jade to stay.'

Cartwright cleared his throat and frowned.

'Is that OK, sir?' said Jade, turning on the charm as only she could do.

The detective nodded briskly.

WIKI

Barry Cartwright stood up and looked at his watch like a busy detective who still had several important cases to solve before he went to bed. 'I'll see you all in the morning,' he said, looking at the adults and ignoring us. He hurried out of the room.

'What a night,' said Pete Bell. He glanced up at his ex-wife. 'D'you need a lift anywhere?'

'I have a car waiting for us,' said Trix's mother.

'Actually –' Trix spoke in a low, firm voice – 'I think I'd like to stay with Dad.'

A cold smile settled on Eva Johansson's face. 'Of course,' she said. 'If that's what you would prefer.'

The parents moved towards the door and we were about to follow them when the same thought must have occurred to all of us at more or less the same time.

MARK

This was it. We had been together, through everything the world could throw at us, and now were going our separate ways. A spell had been broken.

For a moment we stood there under the bright strip lighting of the interview room, uncertain as to what to say.

Jade took a deep breath, and seemed to be about to come out with one of her wisecracks, but then just breathed out. Even she was lost for words.

WIKI

We felt like kids again. We were back in the land of parents, embarrassed, out of place. Each of us knew that we would never be as close again as we had been for those weeks when it was us against the world.

Trix broke the silence.

'See you, gang.' She kissed Mark on the cheek, as if it were the most normal thing in the world, then me. There was a muddle of farewell embraces as the parents looked on, smiling.

Then they left, leaving Mark and me alone in the room.

'All right, Wikster?' he asked.

'Yeah,' I said. 'All right.'

WIKI

My parents were not thrilled by what had happened.

Some things never change.

Forget The Vanish, being on the run, escaping from a smiling psycho. Don't even consider the hundreds and thousands of pounds that had been raised for African children.

I had lied to my mum and dad. That was all that mattered. For days after I returned home, they went about the place with that heavy look of disappointment that must be taught at parent school. Now and then I tried to talk about the memories that were going round and round in my head. I told them about Trix – how she had wanted to change the world. I talked about Godfather Gideon and the birds and animals I saw and learned about at his farm in the Welsh mountains, about Brad and George, about Jaz.

The more I revealed about what had happened, the more worried they looked. They have always had this big thing about trust. Now *I* may have thought I had done something good, but they had no doubt what had happened. They had been betrayed by their only son.

I hid the catapult under my mattress.

HOLLY

Wiki rang several times over the first few days, as if he was trying to hold on to something that was slipping away. He said that sometimes it felt as if The Vanish had never happened, that we had each slipped back into our old life without anything really changing. He was wrong, of course.

It was just that some of the effects of what we had done turned up in the strangest of places.

My mother was unusually thoughtful the day after the Share Awards. Yes, she was interested in what I could now tell her about our lives on the run. Of course she was impressed by how I had managed to smuggle the gang into the Grosvenor House. She laughed when I put on my Eva Johansson voice for her.

But Mum has never been good at hiding her feelings. Something was bugging her.

'I want to help.'

She made this announcement that evening in the kitchen. Jade and I were laying the kitchen table and she was at the cooker, her back to us.

'Help, Mum?' I said.

'Yes.' She was nodding her head as if she had made an important life decision. 'You children managed so much and you're only fourteen. And what do I do?'

Tricky one, that. Mum raises money for charity now and then but has not actually had a job since I was born.

'You look after the house,' I said. 'You keep the family together.'

'Families are tough, Mrs de Vriess,' said Jade. 'Believe me.'

'That's the first thing,' said my mother. 'I'm going to sort out the whole question of where you're staying, Jade.'

'Whoa there.' Jade held up both hands. Although a smile was on her face, there was a coldness in her eyes. 'I'm nobody's good cause, right. I'll get in touch with my brothers. This is a Hart-family situation. We'll figure it out ourselves.'

'She's right, Mum,' I said.

'Well, what about that little homeless girl then? I'm going to help her – whatever you say.'

She was talking about Jaz.

JADE

Mrs de Vriess is one of those scary, no-nonsense Englishwomen who treat everything the same. Organizing a coffee morning, managing a company, being Prime Minister – they're all just jobs to be done.

Before I could point out that she and Jaz belong to such different universes that even thinking of them in the same thought made my head ache, she started to plan. The next day, it was decided, I would take Holly and her mom to Jaz's little home in the park.

What would happen after that remained a mystery. One thing was for certain: it would be embarrassing.

HOLLY

The next day we drove through London to Waterloo. After a bit of driving around, Jade stopped us at a patch of scrubland, a dog's-toilet sort of place. This was the 'park' where Jaz made her home.

It was agreed that Jade and I would go and see her first. Sometimes my mother can be a bit overpowering.

Jade led me into some bushes in the corner of the park. There, in a clearing, was a camp made of bits of plastic sheeting, scraps of canvas and torn blankets. Jade peered under a bush where an old mattress and some dirty old clothes seemed to have been discarded.

JADE

The kid looked smaller and younger than I remembered. Something had scraped her cheek since I had last seen her.

'Hey, Jaz.' As I touched her shoulder, she sprang up, eyes wide, swearing. She relaxed when she recognized me.

'Oh, it's you.' She lay back on her mattress. 'You made it then.'

After I had introduced her to Holly, Jaz told us what had happened that night after her little fire dance. The police had kept her overnight. The following morning, a welfare person had come to collect her. At the first traffic light Jaz was out of there and back into the city jungle.

I told her what had happened at the Share Awards. She was famous. The police would be looking for her. And social workers. And about a million journalists.

She looked scared.

Then I told her about our idea.

WIKI

Some stories have a happy ending.

Jaz was persuaded by Jade and Holly to stay with them. Over the next few days, Holly's mother went into action, talking to the police, to social services, studying the legal position.

It was agreed that Jaz would stay in a private hostel, with the fees being paid by Holly's parents. At weekends, she would stay with the de Vriess family. In the meantime, the police would be looking for her family back in Scotland.

They found her mother living in a one-bedroom flat with four children under the age of ten. Jaz had been right. She was no longer welcome home. There were two many mouths to feed. The lass had always been good at looking after herself, her mother said.

There was no alternative. Jaz would have to stay in care unless someone agreed to adopt her.

JADE

Official: we are now inhabitants of the Planet of the Weird.

Three months after The Vanish gang turned itself in, our unofficial sixth member left her hostel forever.

Are you ready for this? Let me introduce to you Jaz de Vriess, Holly's foster sister.

MR 'GRIFFO' GRIFFITHS

I always say that at Cathcart College caring is part of the curriculum. Although as headmaster I disapproved of the methods used by our pupils Beatrix 'Trix' Johansson-Bell, William Church, Mark Bliss, Jade Hart and Holly de Vriess, I was first to recognize that their 'adventure' had done much to raise awareness of world poverty.

Now it was our turn. When Mrs de Vriess contacted me about finding a place for a homeless child who she had fostered, I was pleased to be able to help.

We would, I informed her, be delighted to welcome Miss Jasmine de Vriess as a new pupil at Cathcart College.

MARK

At first, when Wiki told me the news, I thought it was one of his rare jokes.

Jaz at Cathcart? The brain reeled at the thought.

But it was true. Holly had a new sister and the sister would be in the Cathcart junior school. She would probably have a tough time at first – but then I would make sure that her pretty tough friends in the senior school would look after her.

When I had got back home, I had spoken several times to Godfather Gideon. He was not in the state of mental meltdown which I had expected, and talked more about our stay with him than the unfortunate way it had ended. He asked after Wiki and made me promise that the two of us would return to Hill Farm in the future.

No worries, Gid. Wiki the country boy would not have to be asked twice.

I had also been to see my father for a week in Dubai. He took me out to dinner and talked about how much money he was making. We scuba-dived and drove through the desert. Something had changed between us, or maybe I was seeing more clearly these days.

The longer I was out there, the more I had looked forward to getting back to school.

JADE

I was hanging out with my brothers whenever I could. The Jaz project had taken over at Holly's house and, for all their general lameness, I was missing George and Brad.

You know what? They treated me differently. I was no longer a servant, a chick who did the cleaning and cooking for them. We began to talk about Mom, and Mr Hart, our former father, back in Vegas. It was as if all the crazy stuff that had happened to us – Wiki with his catapult, Trix pretending to be a boy, the mad psycho turning up at the club – had been a wake-up call. It had brought us together in some weird way.

They had decided, maybe just in time, that this was not how they wanted to live their lives.

George emailed our dad and told him about the whole Vanish thing.

And here was another surprise. Straight after he had read about what had happened, in news stories online, Mr Hart invited the three of us to spend Christmas in Vegas.

It was time for his two families to meet, was the way he put it.

There must have been other conversations, because George had decided that he was heading back to the States. There was a job in the casino business with his name (or, officially, Dad's name) on it.

And Brad? Get this. He did something he had never done before: he got a job. A friend of his had set up a business importing vintage sports cars from abroad. The guy needed a salesman.

Pinch me. I think I'm dreaming.

THE SMILER

What about me, eh? *Eh?*

After I was taken into custody, I realized I was facing a jail sentence. You can't stab a man's hand with a broken bottle without the law taking a bit of an interest, you just can't. Even I knew that.

But yet again, fortune smiled on the Smiler.

The American whose hand I had decorated with a broken bottle said he wanted to move on. He had had dealings with the police in the past. He never wanted to see the inside of a courtroom again. He would not be pressing charges against me. What a gentleman.

But my problems weren't over. The police knew all about me. They had a pretty good idea that my hobby in Wales was robbing post offices.

It was time for a career change.

EDDISON VOGEL

There is an old saying: nature abhors a vacuum. Put simply, it means that in life something empty tends to get filled up one way or another.

Fame is like that.

After that marvellous evening at the Share Awards, it was clear that, in publicity terms, we were faced with an entirely new situation. Trixie was no longer tragic but was a charity hero, a poster girl for all that is good and lovely among our teenagers.

We could run with that. There would a publicity-fest, and I was ready to do the circuit with my new star Trix Johansson-Bell and her supporting cast – Eva, the Share Celebrity Mother of the Year, and the other runaway kids (I could see a future for the little American, Jade Hart). I might even be able to do something with the father. The public love an ex-drunk who has been to hell and back.

What did I get? Disappointment. A kick in the teeth. Trix refused all interviews, the ungrateful little minx. None of the other children was interested either. Eva flew back to Hollywood. It was simply beyond reason.

I knew there was publicity gold in this story. It was just a question of mining it.

THE SMILER

A man called Eddison Vogel phoned me. He said he was looking for a new angle on the Tragic Trixie caper. Was I free to talk?

'Eddie,' I said, 'it would be a pleasure.'

We met for tea at the Ritz, which was something of a first for me, I have to admit.

We got to talking. I gave him his new angle – and then some.

EDDISON VOGEL

It was a story that had it all – a harsh childhood, a heartbreaking teenage incident which left our hero scarred for life, a downward spiral into violence, crime and imprisonment. Finally, redemption and hope, thanks to an idealistic young girl called Trixie Johansson-Bell.

The moving, terrifying and ultimately uplifting story of Charlie 'the Smiler' Prendergast. It was a tale for our times.

I could hear the distant sound of cash-tills ringing.

THE SMILER

All I had to do was sit down and yak into a tape recorder for a week or so. Then someone would turn it into a book which would go out under my name.

I'd be famous and get paid rather more than I earned in a medium-sized bank robbery.

Talk about easy pickings.

EDDISON VOGEL

Charlie is a natural. Everybody loves a rough diamond. He is made for the media.

Trust me. This time next year, *Keep Smiling Through – The Memoirs of Charlie Prendergast* will be top of the bestseller charts and its author will be a star.

THE SMILER

Every cloud, eh?

WIKI

When we were into the final countdown before the start of the autumn term, I had had a call from Trix. She wanted to see me.

I told her I was grounded.

She seemed shocked but, with my mother hovering in the background, it was a bad time to explain.

I said something about our seeing one another at school in a few days' time.

'It can't wait, Wiki,' she said. 'Give me your address.'

Early the next morning, a Saturday, she was there, on my doorstep.

I invited her in. My parents were in our small sitting room, my father reading a newspaper, my mother updating her diary at her desk in the corner.

They stood and shook hands with Trix, managing to convey disapproval even as they were being really polite.

'We've heard all about you,' my mother said.

'Yes.' My father smiled gravely. 'Quite a song and dance you led us all.'

'We raised over a million pounds,' said Trix. 'A lot of African children are less hungry than they would have been. It saved lives, our song and dance.'

'So the ends justify the means,' said my mother.

Something in their manner sparked into life the anger in Trix that was never far away.

'I think you should be proud of your son,' she said. 'It's easy to stand by and let injustice happen. To read about starvation and misery –' She nodded at the newspaper in my father's hand – 'say, "What a terrible thing," and go back to your comfortable life. To make a difference, you have to take chances. He was the bravest of all of us. He was always the one who stood up for what was right, who did the honourable thing, quietly and without making a fuss. None of what happened could have happened without him.'

Before my parents could reply, Trix turned to me. 'Is there somewhere we could talk, Wik?' she asked. 'Just you and me?'

MRS GLORIA CHURCH

She was impressive, that young girl. I had expected something altogether different. Her certainty, her confidence that she was right, was contagious, to tell you the truth. It made us think again.

We sat in silence while the children talked upstairs in William's room.

'Perhaps,' my husband said eventually, 'we've been a little hasty.'

We sat on the bed in my room.

'Heavy-duty parents,' Trix said.

'They're all right,' I said. 'It's just the way they are. Thanks for all that stuff downstairs.'

'I decided not to tell them about the catapult.'

'Good thinking.'

I asked her if she was looking forward to the term starting in a few days' time.

'That's why I called you.' She gave one of her decisive little sniffs. 'I'm not going back to Cathcart.'

'You're changing schools?'

'I'm changing more than that, Wik.'

And so it came out. Pete Bell had applied for a job as a foreign correspondent in South Africa. He was flying out next week to start work, and Trix was going with him. Her eyes sparkled with excitement as she told me that she had found an orphanage where she would be able to help look after the children in her school holidays and help teach them.

'Wow,' I said at one point. 'Exit the Trixter.'

'That's something else. In South Africa, I shall be living under the name of Erica Jane Bell. I'm starting a new life under a new name.'

'Erica Jane?' I was about to tell her that frankly there was no way that Erica Jane suited her, but I saved my breath. Trix/Trixie/Erica had never been one for second thoughts. 'It seems kind of drastic,' I said. 'Are you sure this what you want?'

'I'll write.' She smiled. 'Maybe you can come and stay some time – give the children some of that Wiki knowledge.'

'I'll miss the old Trix.'

'You'll prefer the new Erica Jane. I promise.'

Every week, without fail, an email arrives for me at Cathcart from Erica Jane Bell. She tells me about what she calls her 'new family' at the Arms of Hope Children's Home. She has written to Griffo Griffiths, suggesting that Cathcart might develop some kind of link with the orphanage. She is raising money for the children out there. No one out there, she says, knows about her past, about The Vanish, about her life as Trix.

I email back with the latest news from Cathcart. Jaz de Vriess is the new hero of the junior school. Jade is talking about living in America with her father. Holly has been organizing a new Catwalk Challenge. Mark (this was a tough one for her to take in) has spent his holidays working in a sports academy for underprivileged kids. Gideon has invited me to stay in the summer.

These days, The Vanish seems to belong to a different reality. Sometimes, alone in my cubicle, I go over in my mind the things that happened to us. Now and then I take the ash catapult out of the suitcase under my bed. I hold it in one hand and pull back the rubber sling, trying to recreate what it felt like, up in the Welsh mountains, when I took aim at a man's head like some tribesman in a South American jungle.

Then I start thinking about the Trixter. Perhaps somewhere, thousands of miles away, under an African sky, she too is remembering what the five of us did when we were free and on the run during that strange last summer of Little Trixie Bell.

BOY 2 GIRL

TERENCE BLACKER

Is he a girl? Is she a boy?

Sam's brilliant disguise takes comic literature to new heights.

Matthew Burton's life has been fine until his American cousin crash-lands into it.

Sam was only ever a distant rumour, a hippy kid who travels around the States with his wacky mother. Now he's an orphan, dumped suddenly on the Burtons' doorstep.

According to Sam, everything in England sucks, and pretty soon he's making trouble for Matthew and his friends. They want revenge – and Operation Samantha is born. For Sam – small, long-haired and blond – is the perfect secret weapon in the war at school between the boys and a gang of snooty girls. And when Sam sets about rewriting the rules for how boys and girls behave, he discovers an entirely new side to his personality. Soon it's not only Sam that's changing . . .

'I roared with laughter, and wanted to give copies to every mixed-up kid of 11 plus' *The Times*

TERENCE BLACKER

I'm a kid – get me out of here!

Danny Bell's problems can be summed up in two simple words: dodgy parents.

His mum has left home and his has-been rock-star dad just sits slumped in front of the TV all day. So when Danny hears about ParentSwap, a secret agency that helps kids find the perfect parents, he jumps at the chance to try it.

But why does Danny have a niggling feeling that there's more to ParentSwap than meets the eye? Is he just being paranoid, or are the strange things that start happening to him being somehow planned, directed – even watched over?

A funny, clever and action-packed story that is full of surprises.

TERENCE BLACKER

You are about to believe the unbelievable.

Life is good for Thomas Wisdom. Great family, great
friends – even his dog is practically perfect. But Thomas
senses that there is something wrong at home. With the help
of his best friend he hacks into a secret file on his father's
computer and what he discovers takes him on a journey into
the unimaginable – to a place they call The Angel Factory.

Soon, much more than Thomas's perfect life is in deadly
danger . . .

'A gripping and dramatic adventure involving high
technology, deception, intrigue and even murder' *Guardian*

'Well written and pacy, this is a story that just has to be
finished' *Independent*

THE TRANSFER

TERENCE BLACKER

Download Complete. Commence Play?

On Stanley's computer, the brilliant virtual football player he has created stares out at him. Lazlo – a genius super-striker – whose skills may be exactly what Stanley's team, City, so desperately needs.

But there is something strangely familiar about Lazlo. Stanley's heart races. He licks his dry lips. So does the player. Could Stanley's wildest, most dangerous dream become a terrifying reality?

'Compulsively readable . . . in a league of its own' *Sunday Telegraph*

'A superb comic fantasy, blending football, computers and family life into a completely satisfying whole' *Guardian*

'An excellent football novel vying for championship status' Michael Thorn, *TES*

A selected list of titles available from Macmillan Children's Books

The prices shown below are correct at the time of going to press. However, Macmillan Publishers reserves the right to show new retail prices on covers, which may differ from those previously advertised.

Terence Blacker

Boy2Girl	978-0-330-41503-3	£5.99
ParentSwap	978-0-330-43741-7	£5.99
The Angel Factory	978-0-330-48024-6	£5.99
The Transfer	978-0-330-39786-5	£5.99

For younger readers

You Have Ghost Mail	978-0-330-39699-8	£4.99

All Pan Macmillan titles can be ordered from our website, www.panmacmillan.com, or from your local bookshop and are also available by post from:

Bookpost, PO Box 29, Douglas, Isle of Man IM99 1BQ

Credit cards accepted. For details:
Telephone: 01624 677237
Fax: 01624 670923
Email: bookshop@enterprise.net
www.bookpost.co.uk

Free postage and packing in the United Kingdom